He's In My Dreams

Jeanne Hardt

CHAPTER 1

Amber wanted to cry. *Again.*

If her life had just gone on and *ended* while she'd slept, she wouldn't have to endure another painful day.

It took great effort to open her heavy lids. Once she did, the piercing sunlight burned her tired puffy eyes, swollen from the tears she'd shed before falling asleep. She'd earned them—*deserved* them. She had every right to feel sorry for herself.

She flipped off the blankets, then slowly swung her legs around and planted her feet on the floor. A brief glance at the silver walker next to her bed made her cringe.

No way I'm using that stupid thing.

Though wobbly at first, she steadied herself and headed to the bathroom.

Her life resembled that of a baby, but at least she could walk.

It only took eight small steps to reach the toilet. For now, she could get there without help. She didn't want to *think* about a time she'd not be able to leave her bed at all.

God, let me die before that happens.

When she returned and settled back on the mattress, she fluffed the flattened pillows, then leaned against the headboard.

Her room hadn't changed much in the last four years. Luckily, she had the same bed—not one of those awful hospital things they tried to pass off as something you could sleep on. Hard, ugly, and a horrible reminder that nothing about her life came anywhere close to being normal. At least her *real* bed gave her a sense of being ordinary.

The biggest change had been her flat screen TV. She'd be bored out of her mind without it. Her mom claimed it had used up the last of their savings, but she'd bought it for her anyway. Especially after Amber had reminded her she wouldn't have to pay for college.

That conversation had been the cause of one of their biggest fights. But Amber had won the short-lived battle. Her argument had made sense and got her the flat screen.

It seemed they argued all the time. Her mom had become distant, when she needed her the most. If only she could get her to talk about the things she wanted to know before she died.

Even some of the simplest things in Amber's life had become difficult. Pushing the buttons on a remote control would be easy for someone whose hands worked like they should. Hers had become as temperamental as her mom. Numbness in her fingers forced her to concentrate on what used to be brainless tasks. Like managing to press the right buttons to choose a TV channel.

She squinted and focused on the power button, then held the device with both hands and pushed. Her hands shook, but she wasn't about to let something so stupid make her mad. Determined, she made it work.

Success!

She left her fingers on the up arrow until she found the right station. TV had become her source of information. News sucked, but there were shows that kept her going. They gave her something to think about aside from her illness.

Love my remote.

News. *No way.*

Game shows. *Maybe later.*

An old movie caught her eye. She wiggled around and readjusted in her bed, ready to watch the couple on screen fall in love all over again.

She sighed.

Tears pooled in her eyes.

It's not fair.

"Amber?"

Her mom knocked on her door, then pushed it open.

"Hey, Mom."

"You hungry?"

"Maybe." She rarely felt hungry anymore.

"Oatmeal?"

"All right."

The door shut, and her mom disappeared. Another short and *anything*-but-sweet conversation.

She probably wished I was gone this morning, too.

Amber concentrated again on the remote and increased the volume. She sunk farther back into the pillows. The kiss was coming. The one that made the woman go crazy. The one that made her lift her foot off the ground and press her body into the man.

"The one that makes *Mr. Lucky* realize he's gonna get laid." She scowled, then flipped the channel. As much as she hated it, news was safer.

Her personal pity party had been set off by an excruciating doctor's visit. All the pain meds in the world couldn't make it go away. Another miserable headache had started working its way to becoming something unbearable. She rubbed her temples, hoping to dull the steady throb.

Sometimes food helped, but she doubted the oatmeal her mom would be bringing would stay in her stomach long. Food rarely did.

"Okay ..." Sleep seemed like a better idea. She closed her eyes and tried to drift away. "Back to my dreams."

Stupid thing to do.

They'd been horrible lately. *Nightmares.* Even in sleep, she got no relief.

Nothing about her life had been fair. This should've been something that happened to everyone else. A plot in one of those tear-jerker movies her mom used to watch, until reality hit too close to home and slapped her in the face. Now she liked to hover.

Watching and waiting.

Her door swung wide. This time, her mom didn't knock. She came in with a tray of oatmeal, glass of orange juice, and multiple bottles of meds. Typical start to the day.

"Sleep well?" Her forced smile was *so* fake.

"Yeah."

"Good."

If Amber got more than two syllables out of her, it would be a miracle.

"Brown sugar?"

Wow. Three syllables. "Sure."

Her mom sprinkled the sugar, then placed the ceramic bowl on a lap tray and positioned it over her.

"Thanks, Mom."

"You're welcome." She moved toward the door. "Anything else?"

"Not right now."

Her mom hesitated, then faced her again. "Need any help?" She gestured toward Amber's hands.

"No. I got this." *I'm not ready to be spoon-fed like a baby.*

She almost smiled, then started to leave.

Something tugged at Amber's heart. "Mom?"

"Yes?" Her eyes widened, and her brows rose.

The look on her face didn't surprise Amber, but it made her even sadder. Their relationship had taken a nosedive over the past year. Being together twenty-four-seven didn't help. Around-the-clock face time could make the nicest person in the world hateful. Even to people who loved them.

Amber licked her lips. "I'd like to talk to you. I mean ... *really* talk."

"About?"

Did it matter? Her mom should want to talk to *someone*. She never left the house. Had no social life. Conversation with a slug would be better than none at all.

"About ... *life*." Amber's mouth twitched saying the word. It seemed kind of redundant to talk about life with death so close.

Her mom's nervous smile affirmed she'd been thinking the same. "Life?"

"Yeah. Mine. Yours. My da—"

"Not about *him*. Please? Anything but your dad."

"Why? I have questions about him you've never answered. It's not like I have lots of time to find out." Okay, so she probably shouldn't have said it.

Her mom huffed, then defensively crossed her arms and frowned. "I hate it when you talk like that."

Amber had to look away. She couldn't bear the expression on her face.

To get her mind off it, she traced the pattern of the multi-colored quilt with her finger. The blanket Grandma Tyler had made and the one her mom would scream about if she spilled anything on it. "All right. We won't talk about *him,* but will you answer some questions?" She pressed the mute button on the remote.

Finally, her mom sat down. Not on the edge of the bed like she used to, but in the chair beside it. "I'll talk, if you eat." After pointing a stiff finger at Amber's oatmeal, she pulled her thick hair into a ponytail and entwined it with the black elastic band she'd had around her wrist. Always there. The epitome of her weirdness.

I'd give anything for that hair.

Amber grasped the spoon. *Please let me hold it tight so Mom won't take it from me and force this crap into my mouth.*

Another victory. Though she held it the same way the boys used to eat in grade school, she didn't care. She wasn't out to get an etiquette award; she just wanted to manage her own food. Now confident, she swirled the spoon through the glop in the bowl, then shoved a bite into her mouth and swallowed. *Now we can talk.* "Was Dad the first man you fell in love with?"

"I thought we weren't going to talk about him." Her mom's eyes narrowed. Not as horrible as the frown, but still ugly.

"We're not." *Yet.* "I wanna know what it's like to fall in love. Whether it was Dad or not. I don't care. Tell me what it felt like."

Her mom looked away, twisting her fingers into a knot. "It *wasn't* your dad." She laughed. A strange sort of *distant* laugh. "There was a boy in high school. My freshman year. Maybe it wasn't *real* love, but he made my heart pound harder than any *man* ever did."

Amber sat up a little taller. The far-off look in her mom's eyes touched a cold corner of her heart. She'd not seen this side of her in a very long time. "What was his name?"

"Burt Reynolds." Her lips rose *a lot* higher.

That's the most she's smiled in months.

"Isn't he famous or something?" Amber choked down more oatmeal.

"No. Not *that* Burt Reynolds. This one was blond, blue-eyed, and shorter than me, but I didn't care. He was the cutest boy in school, and I'd have given anything for just one kiss."

"Did it ever happen?"

"Nope. We held hands at a movie, but the kids teased him about me the next week at school, and he never asked me out again. Holding his hand was like ... I don't know ..." She looked upward, then sighed. "It was like a taste of *Heaven*. I don't remember a single thing about the movie. I was so caught up in the sensation of his hand in mine—nothing else mattered."

"Holding his hand did that?"

"Yep. My heart beat so hard I thought I'd die. Trust me. The simple things are the best. Forget all that Fifty Shades stuff."

Amber closed her eyes and shook her head. The movie had been the thing to watch. She'd wanted to, but her mom wouldn't allow it. Until she turned eighteen. In four months she might know what all the hype had been about.

No, it'll never happen.

Even if she lived to see the day, her mom would come up with some kind of excuse to keep her from seeing it.

Amber jerked and popped her eyes open, startled by the feel of her mom's hand on her cheek.

"Sorry." Her mom drew back. Her face contorted, almost like she was going to cry. But then, it lost all emotion. "You warm enough?"

"Uh-huh." To prove her point, she patted the quilt. "Did it snow last night?"

"A dusting." She turned toward the window, then glanced back at Amber. "You're not wearing your scarf."

Her mom had helped her put it on before bed, but it hadn't stayed there. *Too uncomfortable.* Amber rubbed her hand over her bald head. "Don't like to wear it when I sleep."

She got a silent nod in response. Did the sight of her disturb her that much? Why should she *ever* wear it? It wasn't like she'd be around anyone who cared.

They'd gotten off the subject. Amber had to get her talking again about things more important than the weather. "So ... what ever happened to *Burt?*"

"Not sure." Her eyes returned to the ceiling, this time apparently in thought. "I saw him at our ten-year reunion. He was married. He talked to me briefly, but I don't think his wife liked it. She made a point of showing me photos of their kids." She grunted. "He's probably still around."

"How long after him did you meet Dad?"

Her mom stiffened and looked directly at her. The smile that had covered her face when talking about the Reynolds guy vanished. *Poof!* Instant anger.

This conversation's over.

"No." She rose like a rocket and crossed her arms, then jerked her head toward the flat screen. "Go on and watch TV. I've got work to do."

And ... she left.

Damn.

She could safely swear in her head. If the word ever came out of her mouth when her mom was around, she'd be rewarded with a thirty minute lecture. It didn't matter that she'd heard *her* string along a series of f-bombs that would make Grandma Tyler roll over in her grave. Seemed it was how she coped with bad news. The worst rant of all had come right after a lengthy phone call from Dr. Carmichael.

Amber shut her eyes.

Please let me sleep.

The pain pills used to work faster. She'd drift off within twenty minutes tops. But her body had become accustomed to them, so it took longer. If only her mom would leave behind the whole bottle.

Not a chance.

CHAPTER 2

Light as air.

Amber stood perfectly still and breathed deeply.

Honeysuckle?

The sweet scent surrounded her. One she'd never forget. She'd smelled and *tasted* them on a camping trip when she was twelve. Before everything changed.

Beautiful ...

Coeur d'Alene City Park had never been so green. It reminded her of the bright-shaded crayon she'd colored with as a little girl. She bent over and ran her hand across the grass—a blanket of lush vibrant blades, softer than silk.

Though she smelled them, the honeysuckles were nowhere to be seen. The air itself held a sugary scent. She took another large breath and found it not only sweet-smelling, but pure and fresh.

She gazed to the far end of the park. The lake sparkled from the sun reflecting off its smooth surface. A sailboat had its white sails raised, and they billowed just enough to keep it gliding across the glimmering water. The tall mountains in the background framed the enormous lake, and the sky topped off everything with a spectacular rich turquoise. The perfect picture.

A child's giggle caught her attention, and she turned to the pleasant sound. A little girl with kinky blonde hair skipped along the sidewalk, following a plump chocolate-brown puppy. A woman, who Amber assumed to be the child's mom, trailed a short distance behind. She wore a cute yellow sundress and simple sandals. She glanced at Amber and smiled, then continued following the little girl.

Amber admired her own clothes. White designer shorts and a matching red and white t-shirt. *No shoes.*

She wiggled her bare toes and enjoyed the feel of the silky grass.

"You have big feet."

"What?" She whipped around to face the rude guy with the deep voice.

"They're huge. For a girl, that is."

She tipped her head, then turned it completely upside down—the only way to get a good look at him. The guy hung from a tree by his knees, swinging like he didn't have a care in the world. "What are you doing up there?"

"Watching you."

"Yeah, right."

"I am. How else would I have noticed those humongous things on the ends of your legs?"

Instinctively, she curled her toes. "They're size nine. That's not so big."

"Nine?" He swayed back and forth, with his arms extended toward the ground. "They look like boats."

How much ruder could he get? She stood a little taller and held her ground. "And you look like an ape." She jerked her head in a fast nod to make her point.

Insult for insult.

He laughed, then grabbed hold of the branch and righted himself. He remained perched on the large limb with his eyes on her.

She gulped. *He's HOT.* Dressed in khaki shorts and a navy blue tank top. And now that he wasn't suspended upside down with his hair on end, it touched his shoulders. A dark mass of thick hair. The kind the girls in the movies always ran their fingers through.

Self-consciously she touched her own hair, then smoothed her hand down its long thick length. She couldn't help but smile.

"You like what you see?" The guy puffed out his chest.

Crap! He thought I was smiling at him. "I ... uh ..."

And just like the ape she'd accused him of being, he beat his chest like Tarzan, accompanied with a ridiculous yell.

"You're weird," she said and started to walk away. Though he'd been entertaining and fine to look at, she wasn't about to let an idiot ruin such a perfect day.

"Wait!"

She stopped. "Why should I? You insulted my feet."

"And you called me an ape." He had both hands braced on the limb. His legs swung freely.

His biceps are huge. Maybe the guy actually *did* have some of Tarzan in him. How else would they get so big?

But even more than the muscles, the tattoo on his right arm had her mesmerized. Intricate artwork. It had to mean *something*.

"Cat got your tongue?" He crossed his amazing arms. "You've been staring at me."

She stomped her foot without thinking. She hadn't meant to stare, but she'd never seen anyone quite like him before. Especially a guy who gave her the time of day. Rude or not.

With a nonchalant lift of her chin, she pointed to the lake. "I was looking at the water behind you."

"Uh-huh." His mouth twisted into a half-grin, making him even finer to look at. "Why don't you come up? The view's better from up here."

"You want me to climb?" Not wise in her white shorts.

"*Can* you?"

"Not in these—" She glanced down and found her legs covered in a pair of jeans. "Sure. I can climb."

"Great." He extended a hand.

"I can do it myself." Effortlessly, she took hold of another limb and hoisted herself into the tree. She faced him on an opposite branch.

"Impressive." He folded his arms across his chest and nodded.

Heat rose from her neck to her cheeks. She grasped the branch a little tighter.

Why does he have to keep flaunting his muscles?

Or maybe he was showing off the tattoo. Being so close, she could get a good look at it. But he didn't give her the chance. She had to turn her head, because he now studied *her* like a fine piece of art. "Stop it."

"What?"

"You're checking me out." Unable to help herself, she faced him again.

"Yep." He nodded with a smile no guy should be allowed to get away with.

Way too gorgeous.

Good thing he couldn't read her thoughts. "I didn't think guys wanted to be so obvious."

He laughed. "Sorry. Couldn't help myself. Once I got past your feet, I realized you're a knock-out."

"Yeah, right." *Who says that anymore?*

"I mean it. You're pretty. What's your name?"

Would it be safe to tell him? She'd just met him, and even though he happened to be the hottest guy she'd ever come across, he was still a complete stranger. She'd watched enough episodes of *Criminal Minds* to know better.

His eyes showed sincerity. Or maybe she just wanted to believe he was trustworthy.

What could it hurt?

"It's Amber."

"Oh. I get it. Your hair, right?"

She pulled the long strands forward and draped them across her t-shirt. "Yep. I was bald when I was born, but Mom's hair's the same color. Guess she thought it was worth taking a chance."

"Nice."

Her turn to study him. Honestly, she hadn't stopped since he'd first insulted her. "So ... what about you? Tarzan, is it?"

"Ha! Girl likes to joke." He sighed. "It's Ryder."

"Ryder?"

"I know. It's different."

"I like it. Any special reason your parents gave you the name? I know your hair color has nothing to do with it."

He shrugged. "Nope. Guess they just liked the sound of it." He looked away.

Things had suddenly become too quiet.

The blonde little girl broke the silence. She raced past them as fast as her chubby legs could carry her.

"Anna, slow down!" her mom said. A soft laugh followed her words. The pretty woman passed beneath them and briefly paused, then continued on after the child.

"She's cute," Ryder said.

Amber narrowed her eyes. "The girl or the mom?"

He laughed. "Both. But I meant the little girl."

"You like kids?"

"Uh-huh. You?"

"Sure." Silence again. She liked his laughter better. As weird and rude as she'd first thought him to be, she'd quickly changed her mind. "You were right about the view from up here."

"I'm usually right." He smirked. The kind of smirk that made her giggle. Not the kind that would tempt her to knock him off the branch and onto his butt.

"The water looks perfect today." She nodded toward the lake. "Almost like a sheet of glass."

"Wanna go for a swim?"

"No." *That's a no-brainer.*

He cocked his head and stared at her. "Why? As you said, the water looks perfect. I bet it's warm, too."

"I don't swim."

"Oh." He hadn't stopped staring. "Well, at least you climb trees."

"Yep."

He licked his lips. "Do you *walk*?"

"Funny."

"Okay ... different approach. Would you like to *go for a walk*? With *me*?" He splayed his hands wide and nearly fell, but recovered quickly and gave her the, *I meant to do that* look.

She giggled.

"Well," he said, clearing his throat. "How about that walk?"

Wow. Persistent.

Before she could answer, he jumped down to the ground, then extended his arms as if ready to catch her.

Not gonna happen. He was gorgeous and interesting, but still a stranger. She wasn't about to let him touch her.

His fingers wiggled in that *come on* sort of way. She ignored them and pushed off from the limb. Oddly, the ground became farther away, and she stumbled into his arms. His incredibly strong, warm, *amazing* arms. If only he *wasn't* a stranger.

English Leather?

She sniffed his neck.

Yep.

Her grandpa used to wear it. *This* guy might be young and hot, but he needed major upgrades.

She looked up and found him peering down at her.

"What?" She threw up her hands and backed away.

"You were smelling me."

"Yeah, right."

"You were."

"Okay, fine. I was. I just think you're a little weird, that's all. I mean ... what guy your age wears English Leather?"

"*I* do. Don't you like it?"

"Does it matter?"

He raked his fingers through his hair. "Maybe."

Wow. I really like his hair.

Sudden boldness made her take a step closer to him. He towered over her by at least eight inches. "You're tall. What are you, six feet?"

"Exactly. Good guess. And since you seem to want to know all my vitals, I'm eighteen. You?"

"Seventeen. But I'll be eighteen soon."

A grin lit up his face. "Awesome. Ready for that walk?"

"Amber!"

A violent shake opened her eyes.

"Mom?"

Her face was drawn up and streaked with tears. "You wouldn't wake up."

Amber touched the top of her head. Her beautiful long lengths had vanished.

Reality rushed in and slapped her in the face. She couldn't stop tears from forming. They crept from her heart to her eyes.

Ryder ...

Chapter 3

Unless she managed to write them down the minute she woke up, Amber never remembered her dreams. At least not *entirely*. Bits and pieces would haunt her—especially if they were horrible nightmares. They'd roll around in her mind, and she'd *wish* she could forget them.

Her dream about Ryder had been different. Every last detail remained. As if she could reach out and touch it. Or paint it into a picture. And unlike the bad dreams, she *wanted* to retain it all.

English Leather.

She shook her head and tried to let it go, then grabbed her remote to find something on TV worth watching. A commercial caught her eye, and she froze. The remote in her hand shook in midair. The model looked a lot like Ryder. Not quite so fine, but he had similar hair.

Amazing hair.

Even though Ryder had started off terribly by insulting her feet, her opinion of him improved the second she tumbled into his arms. If he'd been a jerk he could've taken advantage of the situation and held on tight. But he didn't. He let her go and gave her the space she needed to feel comfortable.

She tossed the blankets to the side and gazed down at her bare toes.

They're not big.

None of her was big anymore.

"Cover up, Amber." Her mom had terrible timing. "You can't afford to catch a chill." She yanked Amber's quilt back into place. "Are your feet hurting again?"

"No more than usual. I was just looking at them. Do you think they're big?"

Her mom scowled. "Silliest thing you've said in a long time." She placed her hand on Amber's forehead. "You're a little warm."

"I'm *always* a little warm."

With a heavy huff, her mom crossed to the window and opened the blinds. "Since you're awake, I might as well let some sunshine in."

"You're mad because I scared you. Aren't you, Mom? I didn't mean to."

A quick roll of the eyes affirmed it.

People assume it's teens that roll their eyes.

"Sorry." Amber meant it. Her mom had enough things to worry about.

"It wasn't your fault. You were sleeping soundly. I probably shouldn't have disturbed you."

You got that right. The best dream of my life, and you jerked it away.

Amber fidgeted with the edge of the blanket. "You're not ready for it, are you?"

"Let's not talk about it right now."

"When?"

"Amber ... please?"

"You used to talk to me."

Once again, she put her hair into a banded ponytail. Dressed in pink medical scrubs, she looked pitiful. Amber couldn't remember the last time she'd seen her in normal clothes.

"Fine." She sat in the chair beside the bed and waved her hand. "Talk."

"Yeah, right." This time *Amber* rolled her eyes. She'd learned from the best.

Her mom grunted. "I hate it when you say that. You do it all the time."

"No I don't."

"Yes, you *do*. Trust me."

Trust you?

She used to. And for all the things most people would consider important, she still did. But she found it hard to fully trust and believe in someone who wouldn't share the most important facts about her life.

Amber didn't shift her eyes from her mom's gaze. "Okay, Mom. Tell me more about the boys you dated."

"That again?"

"Yeah. That again. All I know about relationships is what I see on TV. You've said yourself it's not realistic. So tell me something real."

"You won't like *real*." She folded her arms over her chest and gave her the, *I'm your mom, and I know so much more than you* look.

"You're right. I don't like anything about the *real* I have to deal with every day. So give me something else to think about. Wasn't there anything good you remember about relationships? Other than Burt Reynolds and his incredible hands?"

Her mom's eyes shifted to the floor. She stared at it, as if dissecting the beige carpet with her eyeballs. "I always thought they'd be good, but they never were. They turned into crap no matter what I did."

"Crap?"

"That's the best way I can describe them."

"What about sex?"

"Amber." Her face tightened into a different kind of scowl.

"What? I wanna know. I won't have the chance to experience it myself. Let me live virtually through you. Or bring me a copy of Fifty Shades so I can find out from someone else."

"That's not the right kind of sex."

"Right? Wrong? How would I know the difference? I've watched enough movies to fill my head with all kinds of stuff, but like you said, they're not real."

With lips pinched tight, her mom squirmed in the chair. "Movies are movies. They embellish things. Make people believe they'll see fireworks the first time they ... *make love*." She whispered the words.

Is it that hard to say?

Amber wasn't about to ask. She'd gotten her talking, and the conversation seemed to be headed in the right direction.

Her mom twisted her fingers together, studying them like she'd never seen them before. She cleared her throat. "Good sex is when both people care about each other. Really love each other. Bad sex is when one does, and the other doesn't." A shadow covered her face. "Bad is when someone is just out for what they can get and can brag about it in the locker room."

Amber swallowed hard. Maybe pushing her hadn't been such a smart thing to do.

Who hurt her? Dad?

"Was it *ever* good for you, Mom?"

"In the beginning." Amber had to strain to hear her. "With your dad." She cleared her throat again, then wiped her eyes with the heel of her hand.

Great. I made her cry.

Even so, she'd mentioned him without cursing or insisting on changing the subject. "I'm glad."

Her mom wiped her hands on her scrubs. "And then he left. End of story."

No, there had to be more to it. But doubtful she'd hear it today.

Might as well be brave.

Amber took a big breath. "Did you lose your virginity to him?"

"Stop." She put her hand up like an octagon-shaped sign. "There are some things you don't need to know."

"Then I'll take that as a *no*. Otherwise, you wouldn't be mad."

"It was so much easier before you became a teenager." She stood and looked down at her, more disgusted than ever. "I'm going to fix dinner. I'll bring it to you when it's ready."

"Oh really?"

Her mom threw up her hands and left the room.

I hate myself sometimes.

Snarkiness helped her cope, but it sent her mom off the deep end.

A twist in her belly indicated the inevitable. Could she make it in time? She suppressed the dryness in her throat, and the need to gag, by taking deep breaths through her nose.

Once she'd pushed aside the blankets, she planted her feet on the floor, counted to five before attempting to move, then headed to the bathroom. With one hand braced on the counter, she placed the other against the wall and leaned over the toilet. It didn't take long. She spewed until she dry-heaved.

By now she should be used to the wretched acidic taste, but it tasted as foul as the first time it happened. Ritualistically, she filled a cup with water, swirled it around inside her mouth, and spit it out. She repeated the ritual. This time with mint-flavored mouthwash.

Her mom had obviously heard her, but didn't bother checking on her. Too busy fixing dinner. Besides, if she came in every time she threw up, she might as well add her bed to the room.

Amber tried not to look, but when she lifted her eyes she couldn't avoid the mirror. Sunken cheeks, blotchy skin, bald head. Nothing had changed.

Only in my dreams.

There, her hair had fallen past her shoulders. Her legs had been fleshy and firm. And, her hands and feet worked like normal people's did.

I even had boobs.

They'd filled out her t-shirt. And if she wasn't mistaken, Ryder had noticed.

God! It was only a dream!

Angry, she trudged to the window and gazed out to the street. Whatever snow had been there vanished. November snow had always been unpredictable. The mountaintops were covered, but the city wouldn't be blanketed for another month. Hopefully for Christmas.

My last Christmas.

Of that, she had no doubt.

CHAPTER 4

"Amber?"

"Yeah, Mom?"

Her tentative face peeked around the edge of the door. "Feel like company?"

"Stephanie?"

The only one who ever comes by.

"Yep." Her mom smiled, almost apologetically. "Want me to help you fix yourself up?"

"Sure." If it would keep Amber from scaring her friend, she'd take all the help she could get.

Her mom tied a navy blue scarf around her head, then grabbed the Chap Stick off the top of her dresser and ran it across her lips. She leaned back and gave Amber another smile—a warmer one this time—then tucked the quilt around her. "Let's cover you up good."

So Stephanie won't see my bony body.

"Thanks, Mom."

With a quick nod, her mom walked out of the room.

Amber took a deep breath and prepared for her friend. Her only *real* tie to the outside world. Stephanie always filled her in on the latest gossip.

She glanced down at herself. The blanket covered most of her, thanks to her mom, and luckily her long-sleeved knit top covered her skinny blotched arms. They'd gotten a lot worse since the last time Stephanie had been by.

Stephanie poked her head into the room and lightly rapped on the door.

"Come on in," Amber said, and forced a little laugh.

A Barbie doll lookalike, blonde blue-eyed Stephanie inched around the door then shut it behind her. "Hey girl."

"Hey Steph." She remembered a time in grade school, when a boy told them they were the prettiest girls in the class. At least Stephanie could still claim the title.

She tiptoed toward her. "Can I hug you?"

"Yeah. I won't break."

The hug she received proved Stephanie didn't believe her. "You're so tiny."

"Cancer diet."

Stephanie's eyes popped wide.

"Sorry. I say stupid things sometimes." *I'm such a dumb-ass.* "I'm glad you're here."

"Me, too."

They'd been best friends since second grade and had never been at a loss for words. But conversation had become harder since Amber had gotten sick. Amber *tried* to act like nothing had changed.

Everything's different.

"Oh. I brought you something." Stephanie dug into a large leather tote and pulled out a package. "An early Christmas present."

"Can I open it *now*?"

Stephanie laughed. "Of course. Why else do you think I brought it?"

Afraid I might not be around at Christmas?

Stephanie handed the package to Amber. She studied the thing wrapped in red paper with green polka dots. The small package had only two pieces of tape holding it together, but ...

Her fingers shook.

"Need my help?" Stephanie asked.

When Amber shifted her attention to her friend, the pain behind her eyes made her even sicker inside. She didn't want pity, but she doubted she could open it herself. "Sure," she said and swallowed hard.

Stephanie smiled and ripped it open. "Hope you like it."

Amber ran her hand over the gift. "It's perfect." A Christmas headscarf covered with reindeer. "That has to be Rudolph." She pointed to the one with a red nose.

"Yep. I knew you always liked him. Thought it would look good on you."

"Thanks."

"Still don't wear the wig?"

"Nope. It itches. The scarf's perfect." She left it lying across her lap. "But I feel bad. I don't have a gift for *you*."

"It's early. There's time."

Time. Should I tell her there isn't much left?

"Yeah. We have time."

Stephanie perched on the edge of the bed and picked at the blanket. Her eyes gave her away. They'd gone from looking painful, to glittering with some kind of crazy excitement.

"Steph. What's up? It's obvious you have something to tell."

"Well ..." She shifted around and faced her squarely. "I met a guy." Her poor lower lip got repeatedly bitten, then she giggled.

"And ..."

"He's really hot. A senior. Just moved here from Seattle."

"Big city boy." Amber wiggled her nearly-non-existent brows. With any luck, Stephanie might tell her what her mom wouldn't. "What's he look like?"

Stephanie closed her eyes and sighed. "Black hair, brown eyes, nice lips. And ..." She lifted her lids and leaned in. "A really. Fine. Butt."

"Tight jeans?"

"*Designer.*" She fanned her face, then grabbed her tote. "I took a selfie with him." She pulled out her phone and turned it sideways to expand the photo.

"You're right. He's hot. And his clothes. *Wow.* Boy's got money."

"Yep. His dad's a doctor. Works at Kootenai Medical."

Amber nodded. She'd seen more doctors than she cared to. "Maybe I'll run into him."

"Doubt it. He doesn't work in the cancer center."

"Oh." There'd been no need for her to say it. The huge hospital had plenty of other things people were being treated for. "What kind of doctor is he?"

"Urologist." Stephanie shrugged. "I know. Not very exciting."

"But important." If Amber felt better, she'd probably have made a joke about the importance of peeing, but she wasn't up to it.

"I can bring him by sometime to meet you."

"The urologist?"

"No, stupid!" Stephanie giggled and shook her head. "His son. Jason."

"Jason?"

"Yep."

"Mr. Designer Jeans?"

"Uh-huh." Again the lip bite. What had she already done with him?

Maybe I don't wanna know.

"Steph? Is he anything like that last guy you dated?"

"Luke?"

"That's right. *Luke*. And before him, that jerk Andy. You have a bad habit of finding guys who treat you like crap. You're too nice. They take advantage of you."

Stephanie tossed her head and turned away. "No one's done that. I'm still a virgin." She said it almost like it was a bad thing.

Amber patted her on the leg to get her attention. "That's not what I'm talking about."

"Then, what?"

"They give you compliments to build you up, then talk about you behind your back. You've told me what the girls at school finally fessed up about and let you know. Andy bragged how he'd looked up your skirt when you were wearing your cheer outfit. And Luke swore he felt you up."

Stephanie's cheeks reddened.

"Steph. You said he never did. *Did* he?"

Her mouth twisted. "I told you it was a lie because I didn't want you to think I did something wrong." She blew out a long breath. "I let him. But I regretted it."

"Like I said, you're too nice. You let them pressure you into doing things you don't wanna do. You're gorgeous, Stephanie. Guys will always try things. Just ... don't *let* them. Unless it's something you're sure you want."

Stephanie smiled and flipped her beautiful, long hair. Amber had been taught not to envy, but it was hard to look at her best friend and not feel a hint of it.

"I don't think Jason's like that," Stephanie said. "The first time we held hands, he asked permission. He did the same thing when he kissed me. He *always* asks first."

"I'm glad." Amber returned her smile, and the mood in the room improved. Good thing, too. She didn't want to chase away her only real friend. "So, how's his kissing?"

Lip bite. "The best. And what I love the most is he chews gum before we do it. Gives me a piece, too."

"Nice."

Stephanie's eyes widened. "*Very.*"

"Does he use his tongue?"

Stephanie swatted the blanket, giggling. "Why are you asking so many questions?"

"Because I'll never know what it's like." Instant mood changer. She'd become good at it. "Sorry. But it's true. I try to get my mom to tell me things, but she won't."

"Your *mom?* Trust me, you wouldn't want her to. Besides, she's clueless on how *we* do things. She's too old."

"Maybe. But how different can kissing be?"

"A *lot.* Guys aren't shy. They're willing to try new things. I don't think our parents know *how* to French kiss."

Oh, Stephanie ... I know you're smarter than that. Who will set you straight when I'm gone?

"Steph, I think people have been Frenching for a long time. They did it in *Grease*. And that was in the fifties. Our parents aren't even *that* old."

Stephanie rolled her eyes. "You're talking about that movie you always want me to watch with you, right? Not the country?"

"Yeah. The movie."

"That movie's ancient. It was about the *fifties*, but wasn't it like filmed in the seventies or something?" She shrugged. "Besides, movies aren't real."

So I've been told.

"Steph?" Amber grabbed her hand.

"What?"

"Go slow with this new guy, k? I don't want you to get hurt again."

With an innocent-looking smile, Stephanie tipped her head to one side. "I won't. Like I told you, Jason's different."

"Good." Although not totally convinced, Amber relaxed and rested against her pillows.

"Amber?"

"Yeah?"

"You look tired." Stephanie tucked the blanket up around her, exactly the same way her mom had. "I should go."

"I *am* a little tired. But I'm glad you came over."

"I wish you had a phone. We could text."

Amber grunted. "Not gonna happen." *I can hardly push a button on my remote.* "They cost too much. Besides, other than you, who would I call?"

And forget taking selfies.

With a loud sigh, Stephanie stood. "I still get mad, you know?"

"What?"

"It's not fair. It shouldn't have happened to you."

I won't cry. "Better me than you."

"Don't say that."

"I mean it. I love you, Steph. I wouldn't wish this on anyone."

This time, Stephanie hugged her with every bit of strength in her body. It briefly took Amber's breath. "I love you, too." She rushed to the door and left without looking back.

Should she have begged her to stay a little longer? No doubt Stephanie would have if she'd asked. She'd always been that kind of friend. They'd shared every type of secret. Not only was Stephanie willing to talk about guys, they talked about their parents and their quirky habits. They also shared all the important *firsts*—like when they got a bra and when their periods started.

If Stephanie wasn't careful, she'd probably be sharing another first. Amber was both scared to hear about it and a little jealous of her possibly doing it. Terrified for Stephanie and worried she'd be making an enormous mistake, but also envious that she'd never know what it was like.

Alone again, she pulled the Christmas scarf close to her chest. It didn't take long before her tears freely fell.

CHAPTER 5

Fortunately, Amber's dinner hadn't come up again. It surprised her, since it had been tuna. But not just any tuna fish. Her mom had a way of turning the canned stuff into gourmet food. Even so, it rarely stayed in her stomach this long.

With remote in hand, she lay in bed ready to turn on the TV. Her mom walked in and stopped her.

"What's that?" Amber pointed to the large box she'd set on her dresser.

"Books. I got them out of the attic. They were your grandma's."

"And ... your point?"

Her mom huffed. "You used to read. I thought it would be a nice change from TV."

"I used to read when you were making me do school work, and I had no choice."

"I shouldn't have stopped your lessons." She stood over her with that, *I know what's best for you* look.

"Why learn stuff when none of it matters anymore?" Amber pointed to the box. "I've told you the one thing I wanna know about, and you won't tell me."

"Just ... never mind." Her mom waved her hands like she was washing invisible windows. "It probably wouldn't have been a good idea anyway. What with the headaches you've been having. And ... it might be hard for you to even hold one." She lifted the box into her arms. "Bad idea. Don't know what I was thinking." She moved toward the door.

"Wait. What kind of books are they?"

Her mom looked upward and pursed her lips like an old lady, then set the box down again. "Romance novels. Old Harlequins. Your grandma loved them."

Amber gasped, but then laughed. "Grandma read Harlequins?" *No way.* "Show me."

"They've seen better days." Her mom drew one from the box and extended it to her.

The thin book had yellowed, but the spine wasn't broken, and the pages weren't falling out. It looked like mice might have nibbled on one corner. Still, it was readable.

Amber shook her head. "Really? *Alien Corn*?" She waved the book in the air. "What kind of title is that? And I thought Harlequins were supposed to have hot guys on the cover. What's the deal?" This book pictured a woman casually reclining in a chair. Like a secretary ready to take dictation.

Her mom shrugged. "I never read it. I wasn't interested in romance novels."

"Wanna see my surprised face?"

Silence.

After a loud huff, her mom reached for the *corn* book. "If you don't want the books, I'll put them back in the attic."

"No. I'm curious now. Maybe I can learn something from *Alien Corn*." She did her best to make it sound scary and managed to flip through the pages until she found the publication date. "This thing was first published in 1968. Harlequin released it in 1973. It's really old."

Her mom gave her that disgusted look she'd grown used to. "Your *grandma* was old."

Might as well test Stephanie's theory.

"They probably did things different way back then."

Her mom rubbed her temples. "Some things, yes. Love. Sex. *No.*"

"You mean there might be *sex* in here?"

"Give it to me." She thrust out her hand to take the book.

Amber clutched it to her chest. "No. You gave it to *me.* I'm keeping it."

"Fine. But if you have questions after you read it, ask me."

"Wow. You'll actually answer?"

Her mom crossed her arms, and her disgusted face returned. "You can read for an hour, then lights out."

"Deal."

She left the room shaking her head.

Amber dove into the story.

* * *

"Hey! *Big* Foot!"

Ryder?

Amber jerked around. Her heart pounded so hard she expected it to grow wings and fly out of her chest.

Don't do something stupid and scare him off.

"Wow." She faked a little calm. "It's the ape man. Ryder, right?"

"Yep." He looked around, then brushed his hand over a cluster of pine needles on the end of a branch. "Been looking for some bananas. Seen any?"

"Yeah, right. They don't grow on pine trees."

Of course he knows that. I sound so lame.

He crossed his arms. "You come here often?"

"Tubb's Hill? Sure. Been coming since I was a kid."

And it never looked better. She scanned the area around them. Not a cigarette butt or beer bottle in sight. Everything, *perfect*. Thick trees, flowering bushes, and a smooth walking trail without a single bump or rut.

She breathed in. Clean air filled her lungs and made her want to float.

Not a cloud in the sky.

Ryder took a step closer. "Ready for our walk?"

For an instant she'd forgotten him.

Weird.

Why would she *ever* forget him?

His extended hand begged her to take it, but something held her back. She just stood there and studied the guy dressed in khaki shorts and a tank top, with hiking boots on her feet.

As gorgeous as ever.

Her own boots matched his, but her shorts were denim and her top, a regular t-shirt.

He cleared his throat. "Amber?" His wiggling fingers attempted to draw her in.

"Uh ... Yeah?"

His eyebrows rose up to his hairline.

Incredible hair.

The brows dipped down again. "I don't bite." The way he said it sounded lower and sexier than any actors she'd seen on TV.

Her heart decided to live in her throat. Somehow weighed down with lead, she managed to step forward. Two more steps, and she'd be close enough to touch him— to take his outstretched hand. She gulped and forced herself to move. She *wanted* to hold it.

Time stopped. How long had it taken her hand to join his?

Her fingers tingled. Her heart thumped. His warm, strong hand dwarfed hers and covered it like protective armor. When his thumb moved along her skin, the world tipped on its side.

"Burt Reynolds," she mumbled, and swallowed the stone wedged somewhere between her tongue and the base of her neck.

"The actor?"

"Huh?"

"You said, *Burt Reynolds*. What made you think of him?"

His thumb hadn't stopped moving.

I'm gonna melt into the ground.

"I ... um. Saw him in an old movie."

She'd not even realized they'd been walking. They'd already climbed halfway up the trail that led to the top of the hill. She gave him a sideways glance, and he rewarded her with the most infectious smile she'd ever seen.

His teeth are perfect. Almost *too* perfect.

"You tired?" he asked and squeezed her hand.

Her heart skipped a beat.

"Nope." Even though they'd been walking at a steady pace, she swore she could go on forever. Truthfully, if he kept hold of her hand, she believed she could fly.

Forget walking.

A small clearing opened up in front of them. He nodded to it. "Let's take a break."

"Okay." They came out from the cover of the trees and walked to the edge of the hill that overlooked the lake. A plush bed of grass covered what she'd remembered as always being dirt.

"Perfect place to sit." He let go of her hand and walked closer to the ledge. "Nothing like this view."

Since she stood behind him, she totally agreed. She hated it when he'd released her hand, but this made up for it. "Pretty great from where *I'm* standing."

He glanced over his shoulder and grinned.

Oh, God. Did he know what I meant?

No doubt her cheeks glowed brilliant red, so she looked at the ground. She moved onto the grass and sat, hoping he hadn't noticed. The second her butt met the ground, her hiking boots disappeared and left her feet bare. A green sundress replaced her shorts and tee. She fidgeted with the skirt to cover her knees, then smoothed the material and tried to get comfortable.

Ryder sat down beside her, drew up his legs, then wrapped his arms around them. He closed his eyes and breathed in. "I love it here."

"Me, too." She wanted to ask him about the tattoo, but couldn't. She'd not known him long enough to pry into something so personal. Maybe *he'd* bring it up.

Their hips touched. And when he sat upright and pulled his arms back, the bare skin of his upper arm brushed hers.

Instant shivers. Even with clean air, she had trouble breathing.

He pointed to her toes. "You painted them. *Nice*."

Good. He didn't notice my goosebumps.

"Thanks." Yep. Fire-engine red. The color her grandma used to wear.

"You okay?"

"Me? I'm fine. Why?"

"You're not as sassy as you were the other day."

"*Sassy?*"

He laughed. Another thing about him that sounded perfect. "I liked it. You're quieter today. I thought maybe something was wrong."

Something was more than wrong. The feel of his hand had turned her into mush, and when his bare arm touched her, she was gone.

If I don't get over this quick, I'll run him off.

She butted his shoulder with hers. "I usually don't talk to ape men."

Okay. That was SO stupid.

He grinned. "What kind of men *do* you talk to?"

She gulped. The only man she ever had a real conversation with was her grandpa. A *very* long time ago. Aside from Dr. Carmichael. But she'd never tell Ryder about *him*.

She twirled a long strand of hair around her finger. "I *don't.*"

His mouth twisted into a more playful grin. "Then I'm honored you chose me." He held a hand to his chest, closed his eyes, and dipped his head in a fake bow. "Ape man or not. Hopefully, I can prove I'm worth it." He looked directly at her. His playfulness had turned into something much sexier.

She blinked hard.

Oh, you're worth it. Just please hold my hand again.

She smiled and bit her bottom lip.

"You're cute when you do that." He pointed to her mouth.

"Cute?" She didn't want to be cute. Five-year-olds were *cute.* She wanted him to think she was beautiful. Maybe even *hot.*

"Yeah. But you're more than that."

Go on.

"You're beautiful."

That's the word!

"Let me guess." His brows weaved up and down. "You're a cheerleader, aren't you?"

"Nope."

"Really? You uncoordinated?"

"You don't know the half of it. I trip over my own feet." She shrugged. "Somehow I managed to win a beauty pageant when I was six. It was all downhill from there."

"You could win one now if you entered." He lifted his hand, as if about to touch her, but then pulled it back.

"Thanks." With a quick lick of her lips, she looked away. Something about him tugged at her insides. Just like in the books she'd been reading. Grandma Tyler had some pretty cool stuff.

"But looks aren't everything." He cleared his throat. "I like girls with brains."

"I *read*."

"That's a start." His face lit up with an enormous smile.

Oh, God. He's got a dimple in his cheek.

Could it get any better?

They needed a distraction. She nodded to the lake. "I heard it got so cold here one winter that the lake froze. The ice was so thick people could walk across it."

"I heard that, too." He leaned forward and once again clasped his arms around his legs.

She admired his bulging biceps and caught herself before she sighed.

He glanced upward. "I like it like this, though. Warm. Sunny. *Perfect*." His head turned, and he peered into her eyes. "Wish you liked to swim."

"Nope. Nearly drowned when I was five. Hate the water."

"Makes sense. But what if I stood beside you? Would you at least *wade*?"

Water around her ankles wouldn't be much different than standing in the shower. With Ryder beside her, she believed she could do most anything. "I guess."

"Awesome. I know the perfect spot."

He jumped up and extended his hand. His wonderful, strong, better-than-Burt-Reynolds-ever-dreamed-of-being hand. This time she didn't hesitate. Their fingers entwined as if they'd been made that way.

Not even a blink, and they were at the bottom of the hill. A small inlet with large rocks jutted out from the shoreline. The clear, deep water, a pool of crystal blue. She could see to the bottom and all the tiny rocks that bedded the ground.

"Wait here," Ryder said, then raced to one of the largest rocks. Out of nowhere, a long braided rope dangled from above. He latched on, let out a loud Tarzan yell, and swung out over the water. Somewhere along the way he'd shed his shirt and changed into swim trunks.

Six pack abs.

Her body trembled. He made her insides tumble. She hugged herself to steady the effect, and discovered she, too, had changed. A white bikini covered *some* of her skin. Her curves made her jaw drop, but personal awe vanished when a huge splash sprayed water all around her.

Ryder surfaced. "Yes!" He tossed his head, and water flew from his hair. "That was freakin' awesome!"

She wanted to laugh at his enthusiasm but couldn't utter a sound. Water dripped from his skin as he stepped onto shore. He walked toward her, and sunlight reflected off his damp, dark skin, and sparkled in his hair. Every part of him screamed sexy manliness. She wouldn't care if he *drenched* himself in English Leather.

He should be an underwear model.

He pointed to the rope. "Sure you don't want to try it? It's amazing."

"I'm sure. But why don't you do it again? I'll watch."

Nothing she'd rather do, and much better than TV.

He moved within reach. His eyes shifted up and down, taking in every bit of her. She considered covering herself, but why should she?

I look incredible.

"You have the most beautiful hair." He pushed a strand off her face. "And the rest of you ..." He ran a single finger down her arm. Her shivers came back with a vengeance. "Wow." His smile disappeared, and his brow drew in. "Where did you come from?"

"Huh?"

"Wake up, Amber!"

The sound of the blinds being yanked up did the trick.

CHAPTER 6

"You need to take a shower." Amber's mom bustled around the room with a duster. "Did you forget you have a doctor's appointment today?"

Amber placed her hands over her eyes. "Yeah, I forgot. Why do I have to go? We just went."

And why did you have to wake me up and ruin everything?

"That was a week ago. Dr. Carmichael wants to see how you're responding to the new medication."

"I'm tired, Mom."

Her mom bent down and picked up the book from the floor. "You turned your light back on and read more last night, didn't you? After I told you to go to sleep?"

Could she sound any more hateful?

"I wanted to finish it."

"If I can't trust you to do as you're told, you can't have any more books to read."

"Really? God, Mom! I'm not eight!"

"Don't swear."

"Shit! Damn! Fu—"

"Stop it!" She flung the book across the room, then dropped into the chair and put her head in her hands. Her shoulders jerked, and she broke into a fit of sobs.

Crap.

"Mom? I'm sorry." It didn't help. She cried even harder.

"Mom? I really am sorry. I just got pissed because I was having a good dream." Still no response. "I hate my life."

"Hate it?" Her voice came out as a whiny whimper. She lifted her head. Tears rolled down her cheeks. "How do you think *I* feel? I have to watch you die." She sucked in air. "Every day you get weaker, but you also get more bitter. *Hateful.* I know I'm no joy to be around, but I'm trying. Why do you have to make it so hard?" Every word she said mixed with sobs and sniffles.

"Making it hard on *you*? *I'm* the one dying."

Her mom wailed.

When did I lose all my feeling?

Amber tugged at the edge of her blanket and fidgeted while her mom bawled. A wrench in her heart brought out tears of her own. It had been a long time since she'd considered someone else's feelings. For months she'd been consumed in self-pity. Sure, she'd been worried about Stephanie, but that was different.

She swallowed to moisten her dry throat. "Mom?"

Her mom's head slightly rose. She sucked in air and sniffled, but didn't speak.

Amber had to try harder. "All I want is for you to tell me things about your life and about Dad. Yes, *Dad.* I want to know what happened. Is it so much to ask? One day I'll be gone, and you won't have to think about *either* of us ever again."

"Don't say that."

"But it's true." *Damn tears.* Amber couldn't stop her own. "I know I'm getting weaker. I hardly keep any food down. I don't wanna die thinking you hate me."

"Hate you?" Her face crinkled and she stood. "*Hate* you?"

For what seemed like an eternity, her mom wandered aimlessly around the room. She waved her hands in the air and mumbled to herself. At least she'd stopped crying.

"Mom? You okay?"

"This hurts because of how much I *love* you." She clutched her chest and sat on the edge of the bed. "You're all I have." Her chin quivered, and slowly she reached out and placed her hand against Amber's cheek. "My baby."

For the first time in a long time, her touch brought comfort. Amber's tears became a steady stream that trickled over the top of her mom's hand. "I'll try to do better. I really am sorry."

"Maybe we both need to swear. It might make us feel better." After smoothing away some of Amber's tears, she withdrew her hand but remained beside her.

"No, it wouldn't. You hate it." She sniffled, and her mom handed her a tissue. Amber soundly blew her nose. "Years ago—before I was sick—you'd have slapped me for saying those things."

"Probably."

"So what stopped you this time?"

"Oh, Amber. I'd never do that. Not now. I couldn't."

"Guess being sick has its advantages." Amber tried to smile.

Her mom didn't respond. The sadness in her eyes said everything. She took a deep breath and stood, then grabbed another tissue and wiped her own face. "Want me to start the water?"

"Sure."

"Okay. Yell if you need me."

"I will."

And just like that, everything went back to the way it had been. Her mom started the shower to get the water hot, then left her alone.

Maybe they actually made some progress. At least her mom had affirmed what *she* thought about every day. She was dying, with no chance of remission.

Amber eased out of bed and trudged to the bathroom.

Water around my ankles won't be much different than standing in the shower.

Memories of last night's dream rushed back.

She stripped off her pajamas and tossed them into the corner.

Why's he so real? And why'd he look so sad?

She might have had her answer if her mom hadn't opened the blinds. The way he'd asked where she came from had been so weird. It wasn't like, *hey, where ya from?* But more like he couldn't believe she was there at all.

But none of it's real.

Water cascaded down her body, warm and wonderful. She lifted her hand and stared at it—the feel of his touch still fresh.

It tingled.

Droplets of red mingled with the clear water that pooled at her feet.

"No ..."

She touched her face, then looked again at her hand. This time, covered in blood.

"Mom!"

She tipped her head back and instantly became light-headed. Blindly, she reached for the knob. Her hands shook, unable to turn off the water. The room spun.

"Mom!"

"Oh, baby ..." An arm encircled her, and her mom shut it off. "I'm here."

Amber's legs buckled. Blood flowed in a steady stream from her nose. It trickled down her face and continued to mingle with the water at her feet.

Her mom yanked tissues from the box on the back of the toilet, all the while trying to hold her upright. "Keep your head back. Try your best to hang onto this." She took Amber's hand and held it against the tissue.

With the bleeding somewhat suppressed, her mom jerked a towel from the bar and covered her as best she could. Amber couldn't do much more than keep the tissue in place. "Mom, everything's spinning."

"I know, baby." She guided her to the bed and helped her lay back. "It's okay. You'll be fine."

The tissue became soaked. Solid red. Her mom rushed to the bathroom and came back with a washcloth. "Use this."

"But the blood—"

"I don't care." She held it to Amber's nose.

This wasn't her first nosebleed. Even so, every time it happened it affirmed the seriousness of her illness. An outward sign of the cancer within.

Amber shivered. "I'm cold."

Again her mom hurried to the bathroom, and this time returned with another large towel. She moved it briskly over Amber's body, drying every inch of her. Then she covered her with the blankets and added an extra one from the foot of the bed. Getting into pajamas hadn't been an option.

Amber pulled the cloth away from her face. The flow slowed, but hadn't stopped.

"Keep it there a little longer." Her mom gently pushed her hand back in place. "Are you warm enough now?" Her brow crinkled deep. She perched on the side of the bed and placed her hand to Amber's forehead. "I'll reschedule your appointment. You need rest."

Amber nodded.

Her mom started to rise, but Amber held out her hand. "No, Mom. Don't go. Not yet."

"Oh. Okay." She settled back down beside her.

With the washcloth partially over her face, Amber studied her. Her mom sat there without saying a word, simply because she'd asked her to.

All these years of caring for her had aged her. She'd always been pretty. Amber had seen photos from when her mom was her age and she'd been *gorgeous*. She'd hoped she'd look like her when she grew up.

She doesn't even color her hair anymore.

About three inches of completely gray roots stood out in major contrast to the rest of her brown hair. The wrinkles between her brows were prominent.

Worry lines.

They got worse after Grandma died.

At least when her grandma had been alive, her mom had someone to talk to about her illness.

She had a shoulder to cry on.

But like she'd said, she only had *her* now.

"Mom?" She readjusted the washcloth so her mouth wasn't covered.

"Yes?"

"Grandma's book didn't have sex in it."

"No?" A single brow went up.

I know you're relieved.

"Uh-uh. Just kissing." *I wished there was more.* "I assume they had sex *after* they were married, but the book didn't go that far."

"Good assumption."

"So when did sex become a part of *dating*?"

Her mom laughed. "I shouldn't be surprised by your questions, but ..." She rolled her eyes. "The sixties, I think. Around the time the pill came out. But even so, when I got old enough for *the talk*, your grandma told me I should wait until I got married."

She's opening up.

If it took a nosebleed to make it happen, she'd welcome every one. "Did you? Wait, I mean?"

Her mom let out the longest breath humanly possible. "No."

"When was your first time?"

Another eye roll. "I was sixteen."

"Sixteen? Younger than me?"

Her mom rapidly shook her head, then held her hands to her face. Slowly, she pulled them down. "It was a mistake." Her eyes shifted away. "He was the captain of the football team. The guy every girl wanted to date. And when he noticed *me* ..." Her voice had fallen to a whisper.

Don't stop now. Please tell me the rest.

"I thought he really liked me." *Go on.* "We went out for pizza. He was older. A senior. Had a car."

Amber's stomach tightened. She knew where her story led. Maybe finding out wasn't such a good idea. She pressed the cloth to her nose a little firmer.

"He drove into the woods. All night he told me how pretty I was and how he was the luckiest guy in school. I was dumb enough to believe him."

"Mom. Don't say that. You've never been dumb."

"You're wrong. I was dumb enough to park with him and get into the back seat. It started out as kissing and ... I admit I *liked* it. One thing led to another." Her head dropped. "I was so stupid."

"Stop saying that. You weren't stupid. Did you love him?"

"Ha!" She rubbed her hands across her lap. "I thought so, until he told the rest of the football team what we did. No one looked at me the same way ever again. And then I worried for two weeks until my period came. It was awful."

"I'm sorry." She wanted to reach out to her. No wonder she'd always avoided the subject. "Did you wait to do it again until you met Dad? After you married him?"

"Amber." Her brow drew in. "Do you *really* want to know all this?"

Amber nodded into the rag.

"Fine." She folded her hands in her lap and squeezed so tight her knuckles turned white. "The experience made me bitter. I didn't have sex again until college."

"College?"

"Yes. I got on the pill and did it with anyone *I* wanted to. I called the shots. And after we did it, I dropped them like flies. I didn't care anymore. I wanted to hurt them like they'd hurt me."

"But ..." *This is awful.* "All those boys weren't that captain of the football team. Why take it out on them?"

Her eyes widened. "I gave them what I knew they wanted, then dumped them before they could dump me." She laughed. A weird, sadistic kind of laugh.

I don't like this side of her.

Her laughter subsided into a low chuckle. "One guy even cried. But I didn't care." She stared at her hands.

Amber held the cloth against her nose with one hand and waved the other in front of her mom's face. "That was wrong. You know that, don't you?"

Her mom let out a long sigh and closed her eyes. "I do now. But it doesn't change my opinion of men. Trust me,

Amber. They want only one thing from a girl. Be glad you don't have to go through the pain of finding out."

"No. I don't believe it. I *won't* believe it. Grandma and Grandpa had an awesome marriage. I know they loved each other. And it wasn't just about sex." She didn't want to think about her grandparents *that* way.

"They were rare. I didn't have that kind of luck."

Amber tried to scoot up in the bed. "It's not too late, Mom. Maybe there's—"

"No. It won't. Ever. Happen." She gave Amber that, *this conversation's over* look. "So, I assume that *book* had a happily ever after?"

"Yeah. Stupid title. Decent book. They had their ups and downs, but it turned out good." Amber glanced at the washrag, then wiped it across her nose. "I think it stopped."

Her mom took it from her. "I'll be back in a sec. I need to get a damp cloth to wash off some of the blood."

Amber closed her eyes while her mom ran the warm washrag across her skin. She moved it over her face, then down her neck. "Think I got it all." She smiled, but tears glistened in her eyes.

"Thanks, Mom." Amber took her hand. "You gonna be okay?"

"Me? I'll be fine. I got over all that crap years ago."

Amber doubted it. Her strange behavior spoke volumes. "What about when I'm gone?"

Her mom licked her lips, then turned her head. Within seconds, she wiped silent tears from her cheeks with her free hand. "I don't like to think about it."

"You need to. I want you to start living again."

"What?"

"The last four years all you've done is take care of me. Go out and find your life again. Go back to work. You still have all your scrubs. I'm sure there's a dentist office out there that needs a decent hygienist."

The sadness on her mom's face intensified. "Nothing will be the same."

"I hate to say it, but that's probably a *good* thing."

"Good?"

"What we've got now is *crap*. I'm not afraid to die. For years you told me about Heaven. I believe in it."

"But—"

"I understand you're afraid for me." Amber gave her mom's hand a gentle squeeze. "You don't like to see me hurting. But one day I won't hurt anymore. Right?"

"Right."

"Then it's all okay. I only regret I never got to fall in love. Yeah, I said it. *Fall in love*. That's another thing I believe in, even if you don't. Maybe you should read some of Grandma's books."

Her mom pulled her into a hug. "I'm sorry, baby. I'm so, so sorry."

She held her close, and soon they cried again. This time Amber felt comforted against a woman she knew would trade places with her if she could.

"I'm glad we talked like this, Mom." Amber took hold of both of her hands. "I think we should face this head-on. Fearless."

"Head-on?"

Amber nodded.

"My brave girl." She cupped her hand on the top of Amber's head, then leaned in and kissed her forehead.

"You're brave, too, Mom."

With a tentative smile her mom stood, then crossed to the far side of the room and picked up the Harlequin. "Happily ever after?"

"Uh-huh."

She left the room with the book clutched against her.

CHAPTER 7

The boardwalk swayed from the movement of the water. Amber stumbled.

"Steady now."

A firm grip on her elbow kept her from tumbling into the lake.

"Ryder?" She looked up into his gorgeous brown eyes and batted her own.

"You okay? We have a long way to go." He pointed.

They stood at the start of the boardwalk, claimed to be the world's longest. She'd walked it many times as a little girl. Once she'd gotten over the fear of being pushed into the water, she loved the feel of it. Swaying. Moving with the waves. But completely safe.

"More than okay."

"Awesome." He shoved his hands into his pockets. No shorts and tank top today. Jeans and a t-shirt.

She wore a similar outfit. Jeans, t-shirt, and ... *boat shoes?* Or sneakers as her grandma used to call them. *Wow.* It seemed a little odd. Ryder had on more stylish Nikes.

They continued along side-by-side.

Why doesn't he hold my hand?

He hadn't even tried. After their walk on Tubb's Hill she assumed they were *dating.*

Is he already tired of me?

The calm lake made the movement minor. She couldn't keep from turning her head to look at him—wanted to pinch him to see if he was real. Or maybe she just wanted to pinch him.

More than anything, she didn't want him to forget she was there.

Gulls let out shrill cries above them.

"Have you ever seen an eagle out here?" Ryder asked, and jerked his chin upward toward the birds.

"Not here. I saw a nest once on the other side of the lake. Through binoculars."

"You like to bird watch?"

"Sure." *Anything with* you.

"Cool. Maybe we can do it sometime."

Okay. Maybe we are *dating.*

A couple approached, linked arm-in-arm. The woman's shoulder-length blonde hair glistened in the sunlight, and her sleek white dress looked beautiful on her. Like someone from the sixties. Even her red lipstick reminded Amber of photos she'd seen of people from that era. Honestly, it made her think of the book she'd just read.

As they passed by, Amber turned to watch them.

"Darling," the woman said. "I'd love some vanilla ice cream."

"Anything for you, Anna," the man replied, and kissed the tip of her nose.

Her eyes met Amber's. She cast a knowing smile, then returned her attention to the man.

Butterflies fluttered in Amber's belly. The two of them were *so* romantic. Without a doubt, *in love.*

Amber faced forward again and concentrated on the guy beside her. Could he be as loving?

"Ice cream sounds good," she said with a heavy sigh.

"Ice cream?" Ryder nodded to a bench.

"Yeah. That woman made me think of it."

"What woman?"

"The one we just passed." She motioned to where they'd been, but found no one there. In fact, not a soul in sight *anywhere.* "That's weird. You saw them, didn't you?"

"Sure I did. But hey, when I'm with you, I don't pay attention to much else."

Why was I ever worried?

She gulped.

He's always so ... charming.

"But ..." Amber gestured to the invisible people. "She was beautiful."

"Really? I didn't notice."

"Yeah, right." The way Ryder looked at her brought heat to her cheeks. She spun on her heels and hastened to the bench. As soon as she sat, he took the spot beside her.

A group of ducks paddled by. Five tiny ones followed one large mother bird.

"Look at the babies," she said. *The perfect distraction.* She kept her eyes on *them* and off of Ryder.

"*Ducklings.*" He handed her a few slices of bread.

She stared at it for a moment, wondering where it came from, but then shrugged and pulled off a piece. She flung it into the water. The ducks obviously appreciated the food and quacked their thanks.

"*Babies.*" She pitched another tiny piece in the direction of the ducklings. "I call all little animals babies."

"Okay. I'll give you that." He shook his head and laughed. "Tell you what." He handed her another slice, and his fingers brushed across the back of her hand. "I'll take you for ice cream after we make it all the way around. Deal?"

His large dimpled grin made the warmth from her face spread all the way to the tips of her toes. "Deal. And I'm glad you're smiling."

"Of course I am. I'm with you." He took her hand and linked his fingers into it. "Do you mind?"

"No." *It's what I've been waiting for.* "I like holding your hand. I like ..."

His brows rose. "You like?"

"Being with *you*. I don't really get it, but I feel like I've known you forever."

"You, too."

She swallowed harder than ever. His eyes locked with hers, and her heart beat so fast it made her ears throb. Would he try to kiss her?

It's too soon. I'm not ready.

If she did it wrong, it could ruin everything.

He gave her hand a squeeze. "Let's get going. Ice cream's sounding pretty good." He stood and pulled her up.

Whew.

Relieved, a sense of bravery snuck in, and she rubbed his hand with her thumb. Just like he'd done hers. "Ever watch fireworks from here?"

His eyes shifted to their hands. Did *her* touch affect him the same way?

He blinked a few times, then licked his lips. "A long time ago. Watched them in the rain once. Well actually it was more like a downpour. Horrible weather for fireworks."

"Wow. Sounds like one of the times I saw them. What if we were here at the same time?"

"Doubt it. I'd remember you." He tapped his finger to the tip of her nose.

"I was pretty little."

"So was I. Well, not *that* little. Around eleven."

She laughed. "I doubt you were ever *little*. You're so big!" She squeezed his bicep. "And tall." The aqua sky perfectly framed his dark hair. When they were together *everything* was perfect.

"You're short, but you're exactly what I wanted you to be."

"Huh?"

"Never mind." He gave her hand a tiny squeeze. "I'm just glad to be with you again. I want to know everything about you."

"Everything?" *Not a chance.*

He nodded and grinned. "So start talking."

Bravery plunged, and she felt the need to put distance between them. She let go of his hand and walked toward the edge of the dock. The boardwalk encircled a marina with row after row of boats. Pristine white sailboats filled almost every slip.

"Look at all the fish," she mumbled. *Another great distraction.*

He moved to her side. "Wow. Tons of 'em."

She leaned way down. The clear water sparkled, and schools of fish darted in and out between the boats. "I can see to the bottom."

He rested a hand in the middle of her back. "Don't fall in."

Panicked, she flipped around and clutched onto him. His simple insinuation erased every bit of ease. When she realized what she'd done, she released him and stepped back. "Sorry."

"*I'm* not. You managed to get out of talking about yourself, but I'd do it again if you'd grab me like that."

Not only gorgeous, he's perceptive.

She attempted being coy and tilted her head. "Do you say that to all the girls?"

"There *are* no other girls." He held out his hand, now familiar and comfortable.

As she took it, she smiled. For some reason she believed him about the girls. Maybe she *could* open up to him. She decided to start with something easy. "I grew up here."

"You did?"

"Uh-huh. I'm talking about myself now." She nudged his shoulder and made him laugh.

"Cool."

What should she tell him? What would be safe? "I've never had a boyfriend before." It seemed like a good thing to say. It might help him understand her nervousness.

He stopped walking and stared at her. "Really?"

"Yeah. Really." *Stop staring at me like that.*

"Me neither."

She burst out laughing. "A boyfriend?"

"That's right." He cocked his head. "*Or* a girlfriend."

"I'm glad." She lifted her chin and bit her lip.

Don't know how that happened. You're eighteen and hot.

He touched her mouth with a single finger. "So cute." His gaze changed from staring to something dreamier. She didn't care anymore if he called her *cute*. He could call her whatever he wanted to. She'd even answer to *duckling*.

Her heart pattered and thumped. "We should get going again. Ice cream. Remember?"

"Of course." Again, they locked eyes, then he shifted them to the boardwalk.

She reminded herself to breathe.

"I was born in Colorado," he said as they walked. "Moved here when I eleven."

"Did you like it there?"

"Guess so." He squeezed her hand a little tighter. "But I like it here better. Especially now."

His incredible eyes could easily melt steel. "Now?" She knew what he meant but wanted him to say it.

"Yep. Since I first saw your big feet."

Okay, he could've said it better.

"Ape man," she mumbled, and they continued on their way.

They went up several flights of steps to a bridge that opened when boats were too tall to fit under the archway. That way they could get into the marina.

When they got to the peak of the arch, he pulled her to a stop at the center. He leaned against the side that faced the Coeur d' Alene Resort. "Ever stay there?" He jerked his chin in the direction of the hotel.

"Nope. You?"

"No. But I've heard a lot of famous people have." He studied the tall building as though memorizing every room and wondering who might be inside.

Nodding, she gazed upward toward the penthouse. Supposedly it had a swimming pool inside. "Once it was built, people came here and found out Idaho's more than just potatoes. I was young when my grandpa died, but he used to go on and on about how Northern and Southern Idaho should've been two states."

"Why?"

"Because they're so different. He used to travel a lot. If he met people who found out he was from Idaho, and they said they'd been here, he'd ask, *what part?* Of course they usually said Boise. Then Grandpa would tell them they'd never really been to Idaho."

Ryder chuckled. "I think I would've liked him."

"He was a good man." *And he loved my grandma with all his heart.*

She felt she'd been rambling like an idiot, but Ryder listened as if he actually cared. He was *so* easy to talk to. Since she had his full attention, she decided to talk some more.

"My mom said she ran into Reba McIntyre once at one of the restaurants over there. A long time ago."

"Cool."

"*Way* cool. But I wish I could've seen what it was like before the resort was built."

"Back before we were born?"

Amber leaned against the rail beside him. "Yeah. My grandma told me there used to be an amusement park here called Playland Pier. It had a Ferris wheel and swings that went out over the water. I don't think I would've liked those though."

"Afraid they might break?"

"You got that right. But it would've been so cool to ride the other rides. I love Ferris wheels. They had a carousel, too." She faced him, leaning on her elbow. "You like rides, *Ryder?*" She laughed, but he moved away and turned his back on her.

She followed him and took hold of his arm. "Hey? Did I say something wrong?"

That's what I get for rambling.

He faced her again with a smile. Not so big and bright this time. "No. I get that all the time."

"Makes sense. So, *do you* like amusement parks? Rides?"

He nodded. "I could go for a Ferris wheel. But right now let's go for ice cream. There's usually a vendor in the park."

He held out his hand, and she happily took it.

When she stepped off the boardwalk, she wavered. In the amount of time it took to walk around the thing she'd gotten used to the movement. Dry land felt weird.

"You okay?" He put his arm around her waist.

"I'm fine. Go figure. Not used to the *lack* of movement." She grinned.

"I've got you." His broader smile returned, and his arm hadn't moved. Good thing *he* couldn't feel the butterflies in her belly. They'd multiplied.

Her confidence grew, and she encircled his waist with *her* arm. They walked into the park like a real couple. Side-by-side.

"See." He pointed ahead. "An ice cream vendor."

The little cart sat beside the sidewalk that circled the park. "Your treat, right?"

"Of course it is." He gave her a little one-armed hug.

The biggest treat of the day. Ice cream seemed kind of irrelevant.

Well, maybe it mattered a little. She loved ice cream. And even with only eight flavors to choose from, she couldn't decide. She read the list over and over.

He leaned down and put his face next to hers, facing the menu. "You can have more than one scoop, Amber."

"Oh. Thanks. You could tell I'm having a hard time, huh?"

"You chew on your lip when you're thinking too hard." He tapped it with his finger. "So, which flavors?"

She looked directly at the vendor—a man with a kind face and shining crystal blue eyes. "A scoop of chocolate mint, pralines and cream, and strawberry."

"And what about you, young man?" The vendor smiled at Ryder.

"The same." Ryder gave Amber a sideways glance and shrugged. "It sounded good."

The man produced two perfect cones, each piled high with three mounds of ice cream. He handed them over. The second they took them, he disappeared along with the cart.

She and Ryder walked a short distance down the winding path.

Ryder nodded to the concrete wall that separated the beach from the park. "Let's sit up there." He took Amber's cone until she got comfortably seated, then handed it to her.

She focused her attention on the ice cream. Each flavor tasted better than she remembered them ever being. Sweeter. Creamier. *Perfect.*

She swirled her tongue around the mound of strawberry. "Mmm ..."

"Glad you like it."

"I do. *So* good."

He grinned at her, then attacked his own cone. Her eyes were drawn to his tongue as it circled the chocolate mint. The way he did it made her heart flip.

He stopped, with his tongue mid-circle, and his eyes locked with hers. The smile that lit up his face shined so bright, it should've melted the ice cream.

She returned her attention to her own cone.

Much safer.

"Feel like getting in the water?" He pointed his cone toward the lake.

"Uh-uh."

"C'mon. We'll just take off our shoes and wade."

"I'm not done with my ice cream." *Good excuse.*

"Bring it with you." He hopped off the ledge and onto the sand. "Here. Let me hold yours so you can get down."

She hesitated, but then his big brown eyes took away every ounce of fear. "Okay." What could it hurt?

She gave him the cone, then jumped down from the wall. Her shoes vanished, and the warm sand cushioned her landing. Once steady, he gave her cone back, then offered his hand.

Holding it had become a no-brainer. But the closer they got to the water, the tighter she grasped.

"You don't have to be afraid, Amber."

"Easy for you to say. This is where it happened."

"You mean—"

"Yeah. Right over there." She pointed up the beach about twenty feet. "Mom showed me the spot, but didn't tell me how it happened. All I remember was not being able to breathe."

"I'm glad they saved you."

"Me, too."

This time he squeezed *her* hand tighter.

They'd reached the water's edge, and her toes sunk into the wet sand. She expected the water to be cold, and laughed when it felt more like bath water. The perfect temperature. *Warm.* Most people would probably dive right in.

They waded out ankle deep, then he gave her hand a little tug and led her along the shoreline. They licked their cones and didn't say another word. Just walked along hand-in-hand.

Content.

CHAPTER 8

"Hey, sleepy head."

Amber opened her eyes to find her mom grinning.

What's up with her?

"I let you sleep this time. I think you needed it."

"Yeah, I did."

"When I came in the room, you were smiling." Her mom crossed the floor and opened the blinds. "Asleep and smiling. It was nice to see."

"I was?"

"Yep. Smiling like you used to. No headaches last night?"

"Uh-uh."

Even though the room brightened with the opened blinds, the sky appeared dismal and gray. No sun shining. Drops of rain pinged against the window.

Her mom returned to her side. "You hungry?"

"A little. First I gotta pee."

"Need help?"

Amber shook her head.

I'm not that far gone.

"Okay. But be sure to use the walker. I'll go fix some hot cereal." She left the room, and Amber didn't move.

She closed her eyes and thought about every detail of the dream. Being with him in her sleep seemed no different than time she spent with her mom. Or Stephanie. As real as she felt right now.

She pinched her arm. "Ouch."

Yep, real.

The only thing different about her dreams had been *her.* The way she looked—the things she wore.

And they changed all the time.

In that way, it'd been totally dreamlike. Not only her clothes changed in the blink of an eye, but her surroundings did, too. Everything had been perfect. Spotless. Clean.

So fake.

The other weird thing ... in her dreams, she'd been aware of herself and the real world. Dreams usually weren't like that. Almost like she had one foot at home, and the other in her dream.

She thumped her head into her pillow.

I'm going crazy. That's all there is to it.

One thing for sure, if she didn't get out of bed *now* she'd regret it.

On her feet.

One, two, three, four, five.

I'm not touching that stupid walker.

Steady. To the bathroom.

A moment of fear gripped her the second she sat down. There'd been times it hurt—*burned.* Luckily, she felt no pain. At least not *there.* A dull throb in her head was the norm. Even without knocking it into her pillow. But like she'd told her mom, even her head didn't hurt.

She quickly washed her hands and returned to the bed.

Breakfast first, shower later.

Maybe today she'd make it to the doctor's office. Dr. Carmichael wasn't bad to look at. For an old guy. His hair was kind of golden-brown and his beard and mustache matched. Nice smile, too. If he was single, she'd tell her mom to go for it.

No such luck.

The guy was married, and from what she'd been told, his wife was gorgeous. Supposedly a former *Miss Idaho.*

Her mom entered the room and set the food tray over the top of her. "I made Cream of Wheat today." *Good timing for once.* "I hope that's okay."

"Sure." It looked better than the usual oatmeal. "Are we going to see Dr. Carmichael?"

"Yes. But not until three, so you have plenty of time."

"Good." She moved her spoon through the cereal "I wanna ask him about my medicine."

"What about it?"

"I think I might be hallucinating."

Her mom sat in the chair beside the bed. "What?"

Amber took a bite of cereal, then followed it with a sip of apple juice. "My dreams. They seem real."

"Nightmares?"

"No." *Far from it.* "Have you ever had dreams that are similar? Have the same people in them?"

"I dream about *you* all the time."

"What about someone you *don't* know?"

"You mean like a celebrity?" Her mom laughed. "I've had some pretty decent dreams about a few of those."

"*Mom.*" Amber rolled her eyes. "No. I mean ... someone you don't know at all. That you never met until they came into your dream?"

"No ... People usually dream about others they know, or at least *want* to know. Sure it wasn't someone you saw on TV?"

"Nope. Never met him before, and I've dreamed about him three times already. I could tell you things he said—places we went. He's as real to me as *you* are."

Her mom stood, shaking her head. "That's silly, Amber. Dreams aren't real. They're something your mind makes up. We'll ask Dr. Carmichael if one of your meds could be making it happen. Get him to change it."

Change it? No freaking way!

The dreams were the only decent thing in her life. "No, Mom. I like the dreams."

"But I don't know if it's healthy. You need to face reality."

Wow.

"Reality sucks, Mom."

She got that notorious sideways glare. At least she wouldn't be accused of swearing this time. *Sucks* teetered right on the line.

After a gigantic sigh, her mom inhaled every bit of air around her. "So, what's your dream boy's name?"

Amber was almost afraid to say it. "Ryder." She whispered it, and her heart doubled its speed.

"Ryder, huh? It's different."

"Yeah. But he's something special."

Her mom folded her arms across her chest, but not in a *mad* way. Almost *playful.* "Anything like *Rafael*?" She grinned like Alice's Cheshire cat.

No mystery where Amber inherited her mood swings. "You read Grandma's book!"

"That I did, *darling.*"

Amber burst out laughing. Good thing she'd swallowed that last bite of cereal or she would've sprayed it all over the room. "Did they really talk like that in the sixties?"

"I wasn't alive then. But Dad told me Mom called him *darling* all the time when they were dating. Then somewhere along the line she changed it to *honey.*"

Another memory rushed in from her dream. "A lady in my dream called the guy she was with, *darling*. Maybe the book had something to do with it."

"You fell asleep reading. That'd make sense. It probably influenced what you dreamed."

"Maybe it did. But I never read any books about Ryder. He's totally new."

"Well." She shook her finger. "Don't let him break your heart." She bent down and kissed Amber's forehead. "Eat your cereal before it gets cold."

She left the room. Amber's mind spun.

Why'd I tell her? She thinks I'm crazy.

Of course, she'd just considered it a possibility herself, so why fault her mom for doing the same?

In a lot of ways, she wished she'd kept Ryder a secret.

He'd never break my heart.

Somehow she just knew it. Besides, how could a dream hurt her? The only thing that would hurt now would be to *stop* dreaming.

* * *

"So how's my favorite patient?" Dr. Carmichael looked at Amber through his stylish Lindberg glasses and grinned.

How many hearts had he broken? Maybe being handsome was a plus for a man who had to tell people they were dying.

"You say that to all your patients, don't you?" Amber swung her legs. Examination tables weren't in the least bit comfortable.

He gave her a sideways glance. "I see you haven't lost your spunk. That's good."

"Spunk?"

Yep. He's old.

He laughed, then pressed the cold stethoscope against her skin. "Deep breath."

She obeyed.

"Again."

They repeated it several more times as he moved the instrument around from her chest to her back.

"Good." He held up a light and waved it in front of her eyes. "Tip your head back." She did, and he shined the thing up her nose. "How are you sleeping?"

"Fine."

"Nightmares?"

"No, sir."

"Good."

Her mom had been standing quietly in the corner of the room, but ended her silence by clearing her throat.

I get it.

"Dr. Carmichael." Amber had considered not saying anything about this, but there was no way her mom would let her. "Can the medicine I'm on make me dream things? Make things seem real that aren't?"

"It's possible. You're on a number of medications that have been known to have hallucinogenic side effects. Pain medications are oftentimes the cause." He studied her face. "What are you experiencing?"

"Nothing awful."

Again, her mom cleared her throat.

"I mean ... I *dream* things." Amber gave her the, *are you happy now* look. Her mom stood more upright and, with a satisfied grin, folded her arms.

"But not nightmares?"

"No, sir. Honestly, they're really good dreams."

"Then I'd say it's not a bad thing." He smiled, then sat on his little round stool on wheels and scooted in close. He took hold of one of her feet. "How's the neuropathy?"

She shrugged. "I hate when it feels like someone's poking me with needles, but that doesn't happen very often." The only way she could tell he'd been squeezing her toe was by watching him. She couldn't feel it.

"I assume you use the walker we sent home with you." He peered at her over the top of his glasses.

"Um ... It's beside my bed."

"I see." He stood, then went to the sink and washed his hands.

Okay ... I'm in trouble now.

He returned to the stool. "Use the walker, Amber. I don't want you to fall."

She smiled and silently nodded.

He took hold of her hand. "What about your fingers? Can you grip tightly enough to manage the walker?"

"Sure."

"Okay. Squeeze my hand."

She gave it her all.

"Not too bad." The smile on his face probably made her *mom's* heart race.

"Thanks." Amber smiled back. It honestly helped to have a doctor who wasn't ugly, when ugliness otherwise surrounded her.

He scooted away on his stool, rolled over to his desk, and punched some things in on the computer. Her mom stood in the corner, finally silent.

"Dr. Carmichael?" Amber said, and he turned to face her. "It's the little things that are hard to do. Like working my remote. I just have to concentrate really hard on what I'm doing."

His hands flew over the keyboard. "How's your pain level?"

"Oh. About a three most of the time. I still have headaches. And nosebleeds. Otherwise I would've been here yesterday."

"Yes, Doctor," her mom said. "That's why I cancelled her appointment. She had one of her worst ones yet."

"I see." *Another, I see?* He released a very long breath. *This can't be good.* "Amber, do you remember what we talked about the last time you were here?"

Of course she did. She hadn't stopped thinking about it. "Hospice."

"Yes. You know we have a wonderful facility, and I believe you'd be very comfortable there. It would help your mom. Someone else would be with you around the clock. They'd look after you, and your mom could get some rest."

"No!" Her mom barked the word and left her spot by the wall. "I want to keep her at home. I'm perfectly able to care for her. Putting her somewhere else isn't an option." She wrapped an arm protectively over Amber's shoulder.

"I understand." He sighed. "Mrs. Stewart, step out with me for a moment. Amber, you sit tight. All right?"

"Sure." They walked out of the small room. Loneliness weighed on her as the minutes ticked by. She read every sign. Every poster about diet and how to eat right to live longer. Vegetables and good protein.

Forget that. Bring on the chocolate.

Why bother with healthy food at this stage in her illness?

The door opened. "Thank you, Dr. Carmichael," her mom said over her shoulder. She grabbed Amber's coat from the hook on the wall. "We can go now."

"So what did he talk to you about?"

"It was nothing." She waved her hand. "You know ... our bill. Payment-type things."

"Oh."

Yeah, I know. You're lying to me.

The bill had never been an issue. They'd qualified for some kind of charity program. It had been the only way her mom could quit work to take care of her.

But it didn't matter. Even though she hated being lied to, if her mom felt the need for it this late in the game, then she'd give her that. Still, why lie?

Years ago, when she'd been told she had terminal cancer, nothing anyone said really mattered anymore.

I can't be hurt worse than I already am.

CHAPTER 9

"Like the truck?"

Amber took in her surroundings. She was sitting in the passenger side of a black pickup truck. Ryder held the steering wheel, beaming.

"Yeah." *I'm back.* "Awesome ride." She moved her hand over the beige vinyl seat.

He lit up even more and sat tall. "Sixty-five Chevy." With one hand on the wheel, he turned up the radio with the other.

"The Beatles," she muttered. "I know this song."

"'She Loves You.'" He wiggled his brows. "Great song."

"I agree." Her heart fluttered.

The effect he had on her never changed. But he'd dressed totally weird today. Brown corduroy pants and a fringed leather vest over a button-up cotton, short-sleeved shirt that looked like someone spewed multi-colored paint on it.

Who dresses like that? And who took my pants?

She tugged on the material at the bottom of her top and tried to cover her legs. The insane orange and pink swirls in the fabric were gross.

Why am I wearing something so disgusting?

"I like the dress." Ryder gave her one of his best smiles. Then again, they were *all* good.

"Dress?" *More like a long shirt.*

"The colors are groovy."

"Groovy?" *Okay. Where'd that come from?*

"Oh, yeah." Even the way he talked sounded freaky.

Maybe he'd just watched an old movie from the sixties. *Whatever.* She'd go along with it. At least they were together.

She stared out the window. "Where are we?"

"We're on Sherman. Don't you recognize it?"

Sherman Avenue had never looked anything like this. Not the Sherman she knew. The buildings were like something she'd seen in a book about Disneyland. A lot like Main Street. Every store had been freshly painted and the streets swept clean. Flowers in assorted brilliant colors bloomed in wooden boxes attached to almost every building.

Stranger yet, no people.

"There it is," Ryder said. Though her focus remained on the sights around her, she could hear the smile in his voice.

She faced forward and gasped.

No way.

"Just like Grandma described it." She released the base of her mini dress and held her hand to her heart. "The Ferris wheel."

It rose into the skyline. Behind it, the water glistened. Now it made sense. Somehow they'd gone back in time.

Anything's possible in dreams.

He parked the truck, then came around to her side and opened the door. "Playland Pier awaits us. Let's have some fun."

She put her hand in his and scooted out of the seat, careful to keep the dress from hiking up over her butt.

Why'd they wear these so short?

Luckily her shoes were comfortable. She wiggled her toes in the soft leather sandals. Bright orange toenail polish this time.

To match my horrid dress.

Once she set her feet on the ground, she expected Ryder to start walking. Instead he just stood there and stared at her.

"Aren't we going?" She glanced down at herself, worried about her clothes.

He ran his finger down her hair, woven into a long braid. "We'll go. I just can't get over how good you look."

"*Groovy?*"

He laughed. "I knew you'd like that. I was trying to set the mood."

"So ... you know we're not really in the sixties, right?"

"Are you sure?" He brushed her cheek with his fingertips.

She shivered and closed her eyes. "I'm not sure of anything." Slowly, she opened them and met his gaze. "Except how happy I am to see you."

"You, too." He grabbed her hand and gave it a slight tug. "C'mon."

They almost floated down the street to the pier.

"No way." She inhaled deeply, just to be sure.

"What?"

"Don't you smell it?" She sighed and smiled like a six-year-old. "Cotton candy." Tempted to jump up and down, she decided it wouldn't be smart to do it in the short dress.

"What is it with you and sweets? First you devoured the ice cream the other day, and now, even before we hit one ride, you want cotton candy?"

She tipped her head and batted her eyes. "Please?" When he didn't waver, she bit her lower lip and fluttered them again.

He thumped his chest. "You got me. I can't resist you when you do that."

"Good."

Their fingers entwined, and he led her into the park. First stop, the cotton candy vendor. An old man swirled the white paper cone through the spun sugar, grinning the whole time.

"For you, miss," he said and handed her the pink fluffy candy. He had the same blue eyes as the ice cream vendor from the park.

"Thank you." She blinked, and the man disappeared. At least she still had the treat. She picked off a bit of pink fluff and popped it into her mouth. It melted across her tongue. "Want some?"

"Sure. Though I kinda like watching *you* eat it."

Why did everything he say warm her from the inside out? Unsure how to respond, she took some of the candy and waved it in front of his face. "Sure you want it?"

"You better believe it." He bent down and opened his mouth.

A sudden case of nerves made it difficult to place it on his tongue. Her hand shook. Then one of her fingers accidentally touched his lower lip. "Sorry." She jerked her hand to herself.

"Don't be. But you know if your fingers get wet, when you tear off more cotton candy you'll get sticky."

"I know. They already are. I'm not too good at just popping it into my mouth."

"Let me see."

She held up her hand and wiggled her pink fingers. "When I'm done let's find someplace I can wash."

"Yep. There's a big glob of cotton candy on the end of your finger." He took her hand, and before she could object, had the finger in his mouth. He drew it out, clean. "All better."

A tiny squeak escaped her before she could stop it. She wavered, breathless.

He grinned and put an arm around her. "I've got you."

Yes, you do.

The cotton candy vanished, and thankfully, so did her uncomfortable dress. Capri jeans replaced the thing, along with a fashionable blue top that tied in a knot at her waist. However, one thing remained from the cotton candy encounter. The tingling sensation in her belly caused by a guy with an incredible mouth.

He had different clothes, too. Slim jeans, and he'd shed the goofy vest. The shirt still nearly blinded her, but she'd deal with it. He was hot in whatever he wore.

"Let's check that out." Ryder nodded to what looked like an arcade game.

When they got closer, she realized it was something more. "I've seen one of these in a movie." She peered through the glass casing.

"You like movies, don't you?"

"Yeah."

"Maybe we can go to one sometime."

She liked the idea. Alone with Ryder in a dark theater. It could be fun.

I shouldn't be thinking like that.

"So, do you want to put the coin in, or would you like me to do it?" He held a penny in the air.

"Does it matter?"

"Of course it does. Whoever puts the penny in gets their fortune told."

Her heart thumped. The fake gypsy woman behind the glass with the turban on her head and dangling bracelets seemed to be taunting her—daring her to drop the coin in the slot. "I'll do it. Then you can do it after me."

"Deal." He gave her the penny.

The second she dropped it into the machine, the gypsy moved. She swayed backward and forward. Gears creaked and accompanied her awkward movement. The thing didn't seem to be working right.

But then a card dropped out, and Ryder picked it up.

"Interesting," he said with a grin.

"What?" She tried to get a look at it.

"It says—*you'll find what you lost.*" He handed her the card. "What did you lose?"

Aside from her hair, she couldn't think of a thing. No way would she tell him about that part of her life. She didn't want to spoil this perfect world. "Nothing. Guess that gypsy doesn't know everything." She tucked the card into her pants pocket. "I already found you. I don't think I need to look for anything else."

"You found me?" He touched her cheek, and she gasped. "I thought *I* found you."

She steadied her heart and took his hand. "Maybe we found each other."

With another grin, he nodded. "So ... you ready for the Ferris wheel?"

"Aren't you gonna get *your* fortune told?"

"I'll do it another time. Right now I'm ready for a ride. I've got our tickets." He grabbed them out of midair and held them in front of her face.

"Awesome. Let's go."

A ride attendant bade them forward with a wave. He resembled a younger version of the old guy who'd given her the cotton candy. Same big smile. Same crystal-like blue eyes.

The red leather seat swung after he enclosed them behind the silver metal bar and released it. "Enjoy your ride," he said, then vanished.

She clutched onto Ryder's arm and butted her body against his.

"Afraid of heights?" His brow crinkled. "I thought you said you liked Ferris wheels?"

He cares. "I do. But they still scare me a little. Just when we get way up high."

"Water? Heights? Is there anything you're *not* afraid of?"

"Uh-huh." She took a deep breath. "*You.*"

He stared at her. "I'm glad. I'd never hurt you, Amber."

"I know."

She faced forward, then rested her head on his shoulder. The wheel turned ever-so-slowly and took them round and round. Soft music from the carousel at the center of the park filled the air. An unrecognizable song, but a happy one. A warm breeze drifted across her face.

So peaceful...

When their seat rose higher, the amazing view took her breath. Not only could she see the city park, but also far across the lake. Sailboats dotted the water here and there. The completely green mountains rose high in the distance, full of trees and not a single bare spot.

She took in everything, but Ryder's undeniable presence overwhelmed her the most. His English Leather cologne. His warm body beside her. And the steadiness of his breathing. He'd become part of her. Someone who'd always been there, and who she hoped would be forever.

The wheel jerked to a stop, and she tightened her grip. Their seat swung back and forth until it also fully stopped. They'd reached the highest point. The pinnacle of the wheel.

She leaned forward, peered down, then sat rigidly back. The seat teetered, and her heart raced. "Think it's broke?"

"Maybe."

"Why are you so calm?"

"I'm not afraid. Besides, I like being alone with you like this."

As easily as she could, she shifted to face him. "I'd rather be in your truck. Somewhere on the *ground*."

"Why? It's awesome up here."

"But we're up so high." She craned her neck, afraid to move. "What if we fall?"

"We won't." He took her chin in his hand and made her look at him. "I bet I can take your mind off where we are."

"Yeah, right."

He nodded. "Trust me."

She gazed into his eyes. Maybe that's what he had in mind. She'd forget where they were, lost in his big browns.

A minty sensation filled her mouth. As if she'd just brushed her teeth.

Weird.

"Trust me," he repeated—in a whisper this time.

Her heart pounded.

His hand slipped behind her head, and he leaned closer. Instinctively, she closed her eyes. His warm breath covered her face, then his full lips touched hers.

She gasped. The air became thick. He pulled her against him and deepened the kiss. She didn't stop him, even when he opened her lips with his tongue. The amazing tongue she'd watched swirl around his ice cream cone. He tasted like cotton candy. *Minty* cotton candy.

Wow.

Forget the tingling hand-holding. This beat it by far. Better than anything. Better than food. Or movies.

Even chocolate.

All the things on her list of favorites plummeted to the bottom.

He backed away, but she wasn't done. She moved one hand into his incredible hair and drew him in for another.

He chuckled for an instant, but then his laughter became a sexy, pleasant moan.

I hope we're stuck up here for hours.

They kissed over and over again, exploring the sensation with every part of their mouths. A piece of her she'd not known existed came to life. She now knew the meaning of another language, and her lips and tongue spoke it fluently.

Breathing hard, he drew back, then framed her face with his hands. "You're so much more than I ever thought you could be."

"Huh?"

"I think I—"

"Amber!"

She flailed her arms and jerked from the sound.

Crap!

She might as well have been slapped across the face.

Her mom hovered over her. "You have company."

Amber covered her face with her hands. No doubt the worst interruption since the beginning of time. "Why do you always wake me up when I'm having good dreams?"

"Stephanie's here to see you. And ... she brought her boyfriend. So get yourself together, and I'll bring them in."

"What if I don't feel like it?"

"Then I'll tell them to leave." She crossed her arms and tapped her foot on the floor.

"Never mind. Just give me five minutes so I can wash up. Then come back and help me with my scarf before you bring them in."

"All right. Company will be good for you." She flittered away.

No, what was good for me was kissing. Oh. My. God.

No one had ever told her it was so unbelievable. Not even Stephanie. At least not with any kind of detail. But how could anyone ever describe the sensation and do it justice?

The way his tongue ...

She wiggled in her bed.

What was he gonna say?

She got up. This time she counted to ten before moving. After those kisses, she needed steady feet.

Once she'd dampened a washcloth, she moved it over her face. "I think I ..." She mumbled the words. "Love you?" Could that have been it?

No way he was about to say, *I think I want the Ferris wheel to start moving again.* She was sure he'd felt the same way she had.

Her heart hadn't stopped its rapid thump. So she leaned against the wall and took deep breaths to still it.

Is this what it feels like?

If this was love, she wanted it in masses.

I have to let it go for now.

She needed to get ready to meet Stephanie's boyfriend.

She'd not had a guy in her room ...*ever.* The assortment of stuffed animals on the window bench seat made her eyes roll.

He'll think I'm lame. Or a baby.

Do I care? No.

She'd just been kissed like a woman and wanted more. Her lips still tingled. Maybe if she could get her hands on some sleeping pills, she could sleep until she had more than she could count.

Okay. I'll entertain Steph and Mr. Hot Stuff, and then take a long nap when they leave.

She crawled under the covers.

No guy can be as hot as Ryder.

"Amber, hon?" Her mom's voice sounded sickly sweet. "Can I come in?"

"Sure."

She entered the room, then pushed the door closed again. "Feel better?"

"I suppose. But I'm *not* so sure about meeting *him.*"

Her mom tied the scarf, then adjusted her bedding. "He's just a boy. And Stephanie seems to be taken with him. It'll be good for you to have company."

"Yeah, right." She let out a long sigh.

Her mom walked to the door to let them in. Before she reached it, she stopped and turned. "Be *nice*."

"Huh?" *Why tell me that?* Maybe it had something to do with her grumpy behavior lately. But she didn't stay around long enough to answer her.

Stephanie came in first. Fully made up to go out somewhere. Mascara. Eyeliner. Lipstick. And of course, perfect hair. Her unzipped coat exposed a sweater underneath. Definitely cut lower than what she usually wore. Probably for *his* benefit.

Attached to the end of her arm came Mr. Designer Jeans. Truthfully, he looked like he was holding onto her for dear life. Hadn't he ever seen someone sick before?

This won't be fun.

"Hey, Amber." Stephanie sounded normal. A good sign. "This is Jason." She tugged on the guy's hand and positioned him at the foot of the bed.

"Hey," he said. His head bobbed up and down.

An intellectual.

She gave him a thorough once over.

He's hot, and he knows it.

No longer bobbling like a sports toy, his head cocked to one side, and he stood tall. The deer-in-the-headlights look he'd had when he first came in vanished.

"Nice to meet you," Amber said. Manners had been bred into her at an early age. "You being good to my best friend?"

Stephanie giggled, and Mr. Bobblehead smirked. "*Very good.*" He pulled her against him, then nodded to Amber's *Twilight* poster. "You don't get out much, do you?"

Jerk.

She wanted to tell him she'd not managed to go out shopping for the latest and greatest, and then tell him *exactly* what he could do with her *Twilight* poster. But instead, she gaped at him, speechless.

Stephanie put her arm around his waist and laid her head on his shoulder. "Jason's taking me to see the new *Fast and Furious.*"

Yep. The guy looked pretty fast. But had he met her parents?

Get her pregnant, and you'll see furious.

"What number?" Amber asked. "They up to twenty?"

"No, silly. *Seven.*" Stephanie grinned at him, pawing his arm the way she'd pet a cat. "He's taking me to dinner first."

"Nice." Amber gave him another once over. Her opinion didn't change. "You drive?"

He smirked. "Got a Mustang."

Good. Maybe it doesn't have a back seat.

"Awesome." Now *she* bobbled her head. What else could they talk about? "You plan to go to college?"

"NIC. Then, who knows?" He shrugged.

"That's right," Stephanie said. "He said he wants to go there since I plan to. Isn't that sweet?"

"*Very.*" Amber flashed her politest smile.

It won't last two months.

Stephanie pushed her hair back over her shoulders and Amber did a double-take. *Holy crap! Jason's a vampire!* The sucking evidence blazed on Stephanie's neck.

"So," the leech said. "How sick *are* you?"

Stephanie swatted his arm. "Jace. That's rude."

That's right, Jace. Didn't Doctor Daddy teach you anything?

"It's okay, Steph." Amber glared at the guy. "I'm dying. I have a rare form of Leukemia. If I'm lucky, I'll live to see Christmas."

"No shit?" His head jerked back, and his eyes widened.

"Yeah. No shit." Good thing her mom couldn't hear her.

He jerked his nose into the air. "So, what happened to your hair?"

How stupid is this guy?

"Jason, don't," Stephanie said. "Amber ..."

"It's okay, Steph. I'll tell him." She leered at the idiot. "First I lost it because of chemo. Some of it grew back. Then when I thought I might have hair long enough to look halfway human, I was given an experimental drug that made it all fall out again. And unknown to the specialists, a side effect of this new drug was permanent hair loss."

He nodded, emotionless. "No shit."

With a doctor for a dad he should have a bigger vocabulary.

Amber could be just as unfeeling. "Were you adopted?"

"Huh?" His lip curled like a snarling bulldog.

"Never mind."

Stephanie released him and rushed to her side. "I'm sorry, Amber. I didn't think he'd—"

"It's okay."

"No, it's not. I swear—he's a great guy. What he said was *so* not him."

Amber now had an up close and personal view of the great guy's work.

Where else has his mouth been? Among other things.

"Steph." Dracula spoke. "We need to go or we won't have time to eat."

Stephanie glanced over her shoulder and nodded, then turned back to Amber. "I'll come next time without him. K?"

"All right. Have fun."

"We will." Mr. Sucky Face answered for her, then tossed his head like a superstar.

If I wasn't so sick I'd knock him on his butt.

Stephanie hugged her, then moved toward the door. She walked out ahead of him. He followed her, but stopped and peered around the edge of the door. "You're missing out on *a lot* of fun." He licked his lips and left.

What an ass!

She wanted to scream it out after him, but she wouldn't put her mom through the torment.

Why do nice girls date jerks?

"So ..." Her mom came in the room. "What did you think? He was pretty cute, wasn't he?"

"Mom. No one says *cute* anymore." *Except Ryder. He can say whatever he wants.*

"Oh. That's right. *Hot,* isn't it?"

"Yeah, he's hot. But he's also an ass."

"*Amber.*" Her mom frowned. Luckily, her fussing stopped there.

"He is. And I think they're doing it."

"What?"

"You know. Having sex."

"No. Not Stephanie." Her mom perched on the edge of the bed. "She knows better."

Amber couldn't help but laugh. Yes, she knew enough to get on the pill. The sixties had changed the world—or so she'd been told. Peer pressure and TV added to it. Every show she watched had people hopping into bed on the first date. If Jason had wanted it, Stephanie probably let him, and considering the guy had the, *I'll take whatever I can get* look, Stephanie had *better* be on the pill.

"You shouldn't be laughing." Her mom leaned in. "Did she tell you they did?"

"No. But she has a hickey on her neck the size of an Oreo, and the guy screamed *sex.* If he wasn't from Seattle I'd think he was the son of your locker room guy." Amber covered her mouth. Had she said too much? "Sorry, Mom."

"It's okay. Honestly, I'm glad you're talking to me. No matter *what* we talk about. We shut each other out much too long."

"I agree." *But will you ever talk about Dad?* "Don't say anything to her parents. Please?"

"I won't. I have enough on my plate worrying about you." Her mom gave her a sad smile. "I hate it for her. I could tell she really likes him. She's bound to be hurt."

"And I won't be here for her."

"*Don't.*"

"Mom, we're facing this head-on, remember? Promise me you'll help her if she needs it."

"I promise." She closed her eyes and nodded. "I will."

They sat silently for some time. Amber replayed every look the guy had given her and Stephanie both. Like a snake in the grass ready to strike.

Nothing like Ryder.

Stephanie deserved someone good like him.

Every girl needs a Prince Charming.

After giving her a kiss on the forehead, her mom left the room. Amber shut her eyes and prayed she'd fall asleep, ready to see *her* prince again.

CHAPTER 10

Ryder lifted Amber's hand to his lips and gently kissed it. "You look beautiful."

"Thanks." She gaped in awe at the romantic gesture. It took her a few moments to recover, then she shook her head and gazed down at herself.

Wow. We've gone even further back.

Her knee-length dress made her look like one of those women in an old war movie. Probably from the 1940s. The solid blue dress wasn't *too* bad. Much better than the ridiculous sixties clothes.

"Look at you, Ryder." She adjusted his tie. "What's the occasion? Dress pants, suit jacket, and a tie?"

"The occasion?" He motioned with his head to the building behind him. "A movie."

Incredible.

The Wilma Theater. Perfectly intact. Her mom had talked about coming here as a kid, but Amber had never seen it. It had been torn down when she was a baby.

She'd heard that people used to dress up for movies in clothes like the ones they'd wear to church on Sundays. Like a major thing.

The building looked brand new. Fresh white paint. Clean. Spotless. *Perfect.*

When she read the marquees over his shoulder, she jumped up and down. The dress she wore today allowed it. "*It's a Wonderful Life*! I've seen this before. I have it on DVD."

"Maybe you do. But you haven't seen it like *this*." He put her hand into the crook of his arm. "If you behave yourself, I'll buy you some popcorn."

She swatted his arm and laughed. "Behave?" He'd started flirting, and she loved this side of him.

"That's right. You're not allowed to put your big feet on the back of the chair in front of you. They'll kick us out if you do."

"Oh. I get it. So that means you can't swing from the rafters." She squeezed his arm. "Ape man."

His lip rose into his most gorgeous half-smile.

"So," she said. "If I'm *really* good do I get candy?"

He laughed. "You have a terrible sweet tooth."

She coyly batted her eyes. Something she'd become a pro at.

"Okay." He nodded, then shook his head. "You get candy."

She grinned and followed him into the theater.

The scent of freshly popped corn made her mouth water. The moment she blinked, a tub of the stuff rested in her hands. It glistened with melted butter.

Ryder stood close to her holding a drink that had two straws sticking out of it. "I hope you like Milk Duds," he said, and waved a box that appeared in his other hand.

"Anything chocolate works." She yanked it from his grasp. "Don't worry. I'll share."

"I'm not worried." He parted the heavy blue velvet curtain, then held it to the side so she could walk through.

A long row of tiny dotted lights lined both sides of the aisle, illuminating their way. But since the main theater lights hadn't yet dimmed, they were unnecessary. Still, she couldn't take her eyes off them. They twinkled like stars in the sky.

"Amber?" Ryder cleared his throat. "You okay?"

"Yeah." She blinked a few times, then followed him down the aisle.

Her heart beat more rapidly than normal. Of course, that wasn't unusual around Ryder. But being in this old theater excited her even more.

He chose the back row and scooted across to the middle. The seats were nothing like the ones she was familiar with. No cup holders. No high backs. They were padded and covered in velvet like the entrance curtains, but they weren't very thick. Comfortable enough.

Just like the exterior of the building, the interior was spotless and clean. Her feet didn't stick to the floor. They'd managed to keep spilled drinks from drying and becoming tacky.

The lights dimmed.

"This is weird," she muttered from the side of her mouth. "I'm not used to being in the dark with you."

"Is it so bad?"

"No." Eating became unimportant. All she wanted to do was put her head on his shoulder.

The popcorn and Milk Duds vanished.

He lifted his arm and put it around her, and she burrowed into his body. She found his English Leather cologne comforting. A part of him she wouldn't want to change.

They sat in silence and watched one of her all-time favorite movies. They just breathed together, and occasionally he'd give her a sip of his coke.

All so simple, but totally perfect.

Her grandma had introduced her to these old classic movies. She'd claimed Hollywood had stopped making movies the way they used to. Being in this atmosphere, Amber had to agree with her. Movies used to be an experience. A magical journey. Something special.

Somewhere along the line, they'd become sex and violence.

Amber liked a good thriller just like anyone else, but they didn't make her heart patter like it did now.

She glanced sideways at Ryder. The flickering light from the screen highlighted his profile.

So gorgeous. So good.

He magnified her joy. As many times as she'd watched this particular movie, it had never been *this* good.

Jimmy Stewart and Donna Reed kissed on the big screen, and Amber sighed. Ryder's index finger touched under her chin and turned her to face him.

Her heart pounded, just as it had at Playland Pier. She licked her lips, knowing what they were about to do.

"Amber, I think I'm the luckiest guy in the world."

Could that have been what he'd almost said after he'd kissed her on the Ferris wheel? She shouldn't be disappointed. It was probably too soon for him to say he loved her.

"I'm pretty lucky, too," she whispered. "Not every girl gets to travel through time."

"Are you so sure we are?"

Their faces were only inches apart. "You're always so mysterious."

He jiggled his brows, then eliminated the space between them. He kissed her as romantically as George Bailey had just kissed his wife, then deepened the kiss to something more passionate.

Not so G-rated.

Amber couldn't help herself and raked her fingers through his hair. It begged her to do it. They kissed until the lights came up.

If what they'd said in the movie had been true, hundreds of angels had just gotten wings. The bells ringing in Amber's mind from Ryder's kisses were deafening. He'd put her senses into overdrive.

"Can we watch it again?" she asked with a dreamy sigh.

"I don't think it'll play again today."

She closed her eyes and lifted her face, then puckered for another kiss. His hand rested against her cheek. But when his lips didn't meet hers, she popped her eyes open.

They stood on Sherman Avenue just outside the theater. Bright sunlight surrounded them.

Ryder stared at her. "There's so much I want to do with you. More I want to know about you." He stroked her cheek. "I still can't figure out how you came here."

"Me neither. But does it matter? I mean ... we're here." She shrugged. "Somehow we met. I think it was supposed to happen."

He nodded. "Just don't go away." He drew her close and held her tightly, then kissed the top of her head. "Don't go away."

Amber shut her eyes again, enjoying the feel of him. She'd never felt so safe.

"Ryder ..." She nestled into his body. "You're the best thing that's ever happened to me." She slowly raised her lids to see his reaction, but instead found her pillow clutched to her chest.

"No!" She sat up in bed.

What made her wake up this time? Not her mom. Considering her room was still dark, it wasn't time to get up.

Then she felt it.

Her body woke her, so she could hurl. She threw her covers back then set her feet on the floor. The nightlight plugged into her wall gave off enough light so she could find her way.

She stumbled, then steadied herself by resting a hand on the bed.

I'm not gonna make it.

She grabbed the trash can beside her dresser and dropped to her knees. Just in time to empty her stomach into it.

Tears mingled with the stuff in the plastic container.

He asked me not to go away and I did. Why can't I just stay with him?

"Baby?" Her mom flipped on the light and knelt beside her. "Oh, baby. I'll get a washcloth."

Amber squinted in the brightness. She stayed on the floor, unable to stand.

At least I didn't puke on the carpet.

Her mom returned with a warm rag and dabbed at her mouth. Then she handed her a glass of water. "Swish a little around and spit it in the trash can."

Amber obeyed without question. "Thanks, Mom."

She stroked Amber's head. "You think you're done?"

"Yeah." She sniffled. "But I can't get up."

Her mom moved the trashcan out of the way, then hoisted her onto her feet. "Let's get you back in bed."

Amber sat on the edge, then her mom helped her swing her legs up and under the covers. Once in place, she helped her lay back and covered her with the blankets, all the way up to her neck.

"Don't know what I'd do if you weren't here, Mom."

"I'll always be here." She tucked the edges of the quilt under the mattress, then kissed her forehead. "I love you, baby. Now go back to sleep. I'm sure you'll feel better in the morning." She walked away and turned off the light.

She'd said the same thing for years. No doubt she knew the truth. Each day, Amber got worse.

Better in the morning isn't a possibility.

* * *

"Don't fall!" Ryder's voice shook.

His nervousness caused Amber to jerk. She clutched onto the tree branch and managed to steady herself.

How'd I get up here?

She found herself perched nearly at the top of a very tall tree. Not in the city park. Not even close. They were surrounded by enormous pine trees somewhere in the middle of a forest.

Ryder let out a laugh. "What happened? You had no problem climbing up here, but now you look like you'd rather be on the ground."

I climbed? "You're laughing because I just scared you, right?" He didn't seem the type to find humor in someone's fear.

"Yep. I laugh sometimes when I'm nervous." He smiled this time. No more laughter. "You okay?"

She peered downward. *Way* down. "Awesome." She let out her own nervous giggle. "And yes, I'd rather be on the ground. How'd we get up so high?"

"We—*climbed*."

She hung onto the branch for dear life. This tree came nowhere close to the one she'd climbed the first time she met him. There she'd been near enough to jump to the ground. But here, she hovered at least twenty feet up.

"Why'd we come up here?" She swallowed the huge lump in her throat.

"Remember?" He waved a pair of binoculars. "Bird watching?"

"Oh. Yeah." She gulped. "Why not just walk through the woods? Look up into the trees to see them."

"Sometimes you act so strange." He handed her the binoculars. "You were the one who noticed the nest from the ground. You wanted to climb so we could see them better." He pointed to a tree a short distance away. "Take a look. The nest is in the cavity of that tree. There must be *babies* in the nest. Both the male and female are hanging around protecting it."

His use of her *baby* term made her smile, and for a second she forgot where they were. But then, she teetered, and it all rushed back. "How do you know so much about birds?"

"I read a lot." He shrugged. "You should know at least a little about this particular bird. After all, the mountain bluebird is Idaho's state bird."

"Oh." That was one fact about Idaho she *didn't* know.

She wedged herself into a good spot on the branch so she wouldn't slip and fall, then peered through the binoculars and adjusted the focus. "Cool. That bird's *so* blue!"

"Hmm …" Ryder's tone teased in a way she'd become familiar with. "May be a good reason for the name?"

She lowered the binoculars enough to give him her most smoldering expression. One she'd learned from her mom.

He laughed. She hadn't fazed him.

"The one that's completely blue is the male," he said. "He's prettier than the female of the species. Most birds are like that. Peacocks are a great example. Gorgeous birds. The peahens aren't much to look at."

Amber peered again through the binoculars. "But the female had to lay the eggs. She has all the hard work. The male just has to strut his stuff to get her attention." She lowered the lenses.

Ryder sat a little taller and puffed out his chest. Then he lifted his chin and turned his head sideways, flaunting his profile. As if that wasn't enough, he raised one hand and ran it through his hair.

He's strutting.

She giggled.

"What?" He dropped his shoulders. "Isn't it working?"

"Oh, yeah. It has for a long time. But we're up in a tree, and there's not a lot we can do about it."

"You sure about that?"

"Huh?" She blinked, and they were firm-footed on the ground. She threw her head back and laughed out loud.

Did he manipulate this?

She shook her head. "I have a feeling that, even if I'd fallen from up there, nothing bad would've happened to me. Am I right?"

He grinned and silently nodded.

Always so mysterious.

The birds warbled overhead.

"I think they're glad we're not watching them anymore," she said and moved close to him.

"Maybe." He took her hands in his. "I'm glad to be watching *you*. Male birds may be better-looking than the females, but that doesn't apply to us. You've got me beat."

She stepped closer. "I disagree."

And then, he kissed her.

Nothing else mattered anymore.

CHAPTER 11

Thanksgiving had always been about eating. If Amber could survive this one without puking, she'd be happy.

"Maybe we shouldn't have accepted the invitation," her mom muttered as they drove down the road. "Stephanie's parents would've understood."

"I'm fine, Mom." Amber popped open the glove compartment and removed one of the blue plastic carsick bags and waved it in the air. "I have this for the ride home."

"I hope you won't need it."

She turned into the Smiths' driveway. Their house had already been decorated for Christmas. Icicle lights hung from the eaves. Though they were lit, they gave off very little light. Not dark enough yet. By the time they left, they'd probably be pretty.

Her mom shut off the motor, then sat, unmoving.

"What's wrong, Mom?"

"I don't know if I can do this."

"Why? I know you like Stephanie's parents."

"Yes, I do." She gripped the steering wheel and twisted her hands around it. It squeaked under her fingers. "But I'm not much good at small talk these days."

Amber placed her hand on top of her mom's. "It's okay. They'll understand. I'm sure they'll make it easy on us. I'm really glad we came. We both need to get out of the house every now and then."

Her mom shifted in the seat and looked her in the eye. "When did you become the grownup?"

Amber shrugged. "I had a good teacher." She jerked her head toward the door. "C'mon. I'll need your help to get out of the van."

Because Amber didn't want to be seen in public with it, she'd insisted they leave the walker at home. Her mom had finally agreed to it, only after Amber promised she'd not try to maneuver around the Smith's house without help from someone.

Her mom opened the car door, undid her seatbelt, and helped her to the ground. Before they started walking, they stood still for a moment. A ritual they both knew well. Then Amber linked her arm into her mom's, and they made their way up the winding concrete path.

"Good thing they only have three steps," Amber said, nodding to the obstacle ahead.

"Yep." Her mom tightened her grip, and they took them one at a time. "You warm enough?"

"I'm fine." Not only had she worn jeans and a heavy sweater, but also had on a long wool coat, scarf, and gloves. She'd decided to wear the Rudolph headscarf from Stephanie, even with Christmas a month away. Amber knew it would make her happy.

Her mom placed a hand to her forehead. "Be sure to let me know if you catch a chill."

"I will."

Before they had a chance to push the doorbell, the door opened wide.

"Happy Thanksgiving!" Mrs. Smith chimed louder than any bell. *Kimberly* Smith, the adult version of Stephanie. She'd even kept *her* Barbie doll figure. "Come in!"

The instant they stepped inside, the aroma of incredible food filled the air. Better yet, it didn't churn Amber's stomach. Maybe she could actually enjoy some of it.

And then Mr. Smith approached. *Don* Smith. Attorney extraordinaire. Not someone to mess with. Not only incredibly smart, but big. At least six-five and probably two-hundred and fifty pounds. An intimidating presence in any courtroom.

I bet Jason hasn't met him yet.

"Glad you could make it," he said, in his attorney bass. "Amber, you look wonderful. And so do you, Carol."

It sounded totally weird hearing someone call her mom by her first name. But it made sense. They'd been friends a long time. Went to high school together.

"Thank you," her mom said, before she could utter a word. "We appreciate the invitation. Don't we, Amber?"

"Yes, we do. Thanks."

Amber glimpsed someone's head darting behind the door down the hallway. A giggle confirmed who it was. Tamara, Stephanie's ten-year-old sister.

I hope they told her about me.

If the girl hadn't been forewarned, it could make for interesting dinner conversation. Kids always spoke their minds. Maybe that was Jason's problem. He was a six-year-old boy in the body of someone eighteen with raging hormones.

"Amber!" Stephanie bounded into the hallway and hugged her tight. Seemed she no longer feared breaking her.

"Hey, Steph. Happy Thanksgiving."

"You, too." She linked her arm through Amber's. "Mom, is it okay if I take Amber to my room until dinner's ready?"

"Of course." Mrs. Smith smiled, then turned to her mom for approval.

"Fine by me," she said. "As long as Stephanie helps her."

"No prob!" Stephanie took a firm hold on Amber's arm and led her down the hall to her room.

The girl must have OD'd on sugar. Luckily, she had enough sense to go slowly, but nervous energy bounced off her and made *Amber's* body shake.

She took Amber's coat, helped her to a chair, then closed the bedroom door.

"What's with you, Steph?" Now coatless, an instant chill in the air caused Amber to shiver.

Stephanie hugged herself and spun in a circle. With a loud sigh, she plopped down onto her back in the middle of the bed. "I'm *so* in love!"

Oh, God …

"In love?" Amber almost hated to ask.

"More than I thought was possible." She writhed around—kind of like a fish out of water, but a lot more disgusting—then sat upright. "Jason's so incredible. I don't know how I got so lucky. He's sweet and sexy. And—"

"Steph." Amber couldn't let her continue. "The guy has issues."

Stephanie shook her head and waved her hand. "You don't know him like I do. The other day he was just anxious to get to the restaurant. He was afraid we wouldn't have time to eat. And—I don't want you to feel bad—but he was kind of freaked out around you. That's why he wasn't himself."

Yeah, love is blind, and she needs a Seeing Eye dog.

The reason the girl always got hurt.

"He was rude, Steph. *Unfeeling.* I know you like the guy, but you shouldn't have to make excuses for him."

Stephanie hopped off the bed, knelt in front of her, and took her hands. "I don't just *like* him, Amber. I really think

I love him." She stared straight into Amber's eyes. "I swear. He treats me great. He's different than my other boyfriends. Nothing like Luke and Andy."

"He's not pressuring you to do things, is he?"

She bit her bottom lip. "Uh-uh. We kiss and stuff, but that's all."

It was the *and stuff* that had Amber worried. She let go of Stephanie's hands and pushed aside the hair at her neck. "Your hickey's almost gone."

Stephanie quickly covered the spot. "You saw it?"

"Hard to miss. I thought for sure you two were doing more than kissing. I mean ... C'mon, Steph."

"Well ..." Stephanie twisted her mouth. "He just got a little carried away."

"Right. Our vacuum cleaner couldn't suck hard enough to leave a mark like that."

Stephanie giggled.

Amber sighed, frustrated at herself for making a joke when her best friend's future was headed downhill. "I worry about you. Just remember what I told you. Don't feel you have to do something just because he wants you to. No guy's worth doing things you'll regret." She shivered again. "Steph, I'm kinda cold. Can you give me my coat?"

"Sure." She jumped up from the floor and handed it to her. "You're really pale."

"I'm fine." Amber draped the coat over her lap and huddled beneath it.

Stephanie perched on the edge of her bed. "You spend too much time worrying about me. You should be worried about yourself."

"I don't need to worry about myself. I know what's gonna happen to me. But you ..." She looked Stephanie in the eye. "You're too nice, and someday I won't be here to bail you out of all the messes you get yourself into."

"You keep saying shit like that, and I don't like it." Stephanie leaned back on her elbows. Her mood had taken a dive.

"What? You don't like me to point out that you get yourself into crap, or that I won't be here to help you get out of it?"

"Both." She sat up again. Her smile returned as fast as it had vanished. "You're my best friend, and I trust your opinion. But you're wrong about Jason. So ... let's talk about something good. Not *just* Jason."

There'd been nothing good about the guy that Amber had seen. Well, he *looked* good, but beyond that—not one thing.

Do I dare?

The instant Stephanie had mentioned something good; a particular person had come to mind.

Amber pulled the coat tighter around her. "Steph, I wanna tell you something, but I don't want you to think I'm weird."

Stephanie repositioned herself on the bed and sat cross-legged. "I won't. You can tell me anything."

"What if I told you *I've* been kissed?"

"Oh. My. God! Who?" She leaned in, eyes bigger than doughnuts.

"No one you know."

"But how? I mean ... it's not like you get out." Seemed Jason had worn off on her. He'd said almost the same thing.

Amber questioned her decision to say something, but she had to convince Stephanie she could find someone better out there than Jason. "He's in my dreams."

Stephanie rolled her eyes. "Really, Amber? For a second I believed you. Don't do that to me."

"I'm serious. I dream about him all the time. The dreams are real to me. I see him, touch him ..." She laughed. "I even smell him."

"Okay. Now *that's* weird."

"I know. He wears English Leather."

Stephanie stared at her like she'd totally lost it. "Is he an old guy or something?"

"No. He's eighteen. And *hot*."

"As hot as Jason?"

Amber couldn't keep from grinning. "*Hotter*."

"No. Way." Stephanie tipped her head to the side. "You said you touched him. How?"

Amber closed her eyes and pictured him. "We've held hands. He's had his arm around me. And like I told you, we've kissed. It was awesome."

"Tongue?"

Amber burst out laughing. "You're getting back at me now, aren't you?"

"It's only fair. So tell me."

"Yeah. Tongue. *Great* tongue."

Stephanie crossed her arms. "I still don't think it counts. I mean ... dreams aren't real. But I'm glad you had virtual tongue." She giggled. "So ... if your dream guy wants more, will you let him?"

"He's not like that."

"No?"

Thoughts of Ryder drifted through her mind. "He's so good. I know he really cares about me. He'd never hurt me. And he wouldn't push me to do something I'm not ready for."

"It sounds to me like your dream lover is a lot like Jason. I'm happy for you, Amber. Good dreams probably make up for some of the shit you have to deal with."

"True. My nights are way better than my days."

A knock on the door turned their heads.

Tamara peeked around the doorframe. "Mom says dinner's ready."

"K," Stephanie said. "Tell her we'll be right there." She extended her hand to Amber. "C'mon girlfriend. Mom doesn't like the food to get cold."

"Just like *my* mom." Amber stood and latched onto Stephanie's arm. "Don't say anything about what I told you, k?"

"It'll be our secret. Like lots of other stuff."

"Thanks."

The dining room had been set with expensive-looking china and crystal drinking glasses. It had been so perfectly put together, it seemed like a crime to mess it up. Everything had been arranged on a carved wood table. It reminded her of something she'd seen in one of her mom's food magazines. Tons of food had already been set out, dished up in fancy bowls. A perfectly-browned turkey sat in the center, partially carved.

"Amber?" Her mom rushed to her side. "Are you okay? You're pale."

"I told her the same thing, Mrs. Stewart," Stephanie said. "She said she was cold."

"Baby? You're cold?"

"I'm fine, Mom. I just got a little chill, so I put my coat back on."

"I'll get a throw," Mrs. Smith said, and bustled out of the room.

Amber hated being fussed over. Stephanie guided her to a chair at the end of the table, and Mr. Smith helped her sit. By the time her butt hit the chair, Mrs. Smith had come back with the fleece throw. She draped it over Amber's legs.

"There," Mrs. Smith said. "Better?"

"Yes. Thank you." Every face in the room gaped at her. Her stomach turned flip-flops.

Please, not now.

She took deep breaths through her nose and attempted to stop the nauseating feeling before it got worse.

After everyone sat, Mr. Smith offered a short but decent blessing, then they passed the food around. Amber's mom treated her like a baby and spooned dabs of it onto her plate. Probably for the best. The bowls were likely heavy. Luckily, she only gave her small portions.

Amber took tiny bites. The mashed potatoes went down the easiest. She nibbled at the other things, then got a gut feeling she was being watched. Her gaze met Tamara's, and the girl quickly looked away. Seemed her curiosity had gotten the best of her.

Tamara giggled, perfectly holding her fork. *She must think it's weird I'm holding mine like a shovel.*

"So, Tamara." Amber decided to make the first move. "How do you like school this year?"

"It's okay." The girl chased peas around her plate with her poised fork. "Is that scarf the one Stephanie gave you?"

"Yes. I know it's not quite Christmas, but I like it."

"But ..." Tamara's mouth twisted, then she wrinkled her nose. "I thought people like you wore wigs. Why don't *you* wear one?"

"Tamara." Mrs. Smith scolded her, simply by saying her name.

"It's okay, Mrs. Smith," Amber said. "I don't mind answering her." She looked directly at the girl. "I have a wig, but it itches. It doesn't feel good on my head. So I wear scarves."

"Oh." Tamara again glanced at her mom, but then sat up tall and stared at Amber. "Does cancer hurt?"

Dead silence followed gasps from every adult at the table. Not even the sound of chewing.

"A little." Amber jumped right in before the girl got a much worse reprimand. "But the doctor gives me medicine so it doesn't hurt so bad."

"That's good. Isn't it, Mom?"

Mrs. Smith nodded. "Yes, it's very good."

"You're seeing Dr. Carmichael, aren't you?" Mr. Smith asked.

"Yes, she is." For some unexplained reason, this time her mom felt the need to answer for her. "We had a promising visit with him recently."

"Does that mean she's not gonna die?" Tamara asked.

Mrs. Smith's eyes widened. The mortified woman scooted back from the table, grabbed Tamara by the arm, and pulled her down the hallway. Tamara whined the entire way. A door shut, and the little girl's simpering cry followed.

"No," Amber said. "Please ... she shouldn't be in trouble for asking questions." She turned to Mr. Smith for help. "Please, go tell your wife that what she said didn't bother me."

He stood. "It was uncalled for. I'll tell her, but I doubt we'll allow her to return to the table. I thought we'd taught her manners." Frowning, he looked across the table. "I'm sorry, Carol."

"It's all right," her mom said. "She's a little girl who didn't know better. Please don't punish her."

Stephanie wiped her mouth with a cloth napkin, then tossed it onto the table. "She's so stupid. I'm sorry, Amber."

"It's really okay. I mean, doctors are supposed to make people better. I don't think she asked anything wrong." She shivered. Even the lap throw hadn't helped. "It think it's gonna snow. I'm freezing."

Her mom placed a ritualistic hand to Amber's forehead. "You're warmer than normal. We should go." She pushed back her chair and stood. The second the Smiths returned, she told them they needed to leave.

Amber was more than ready. She couldn't stop shaking, and the food she'd eaten threatened to come up again.

After a round of friendly hugs, and a foil-wrapped plate of pumpkin pie for later, they headed back home.

"I'm sorry," Amber said. A carsick bag lay in her lap ready to be used. She held her hands up to the heat blowing from the vents.

"Don't be. We gave it a good try." Her mom kept her eyes glued to the road. "I'll just be glad to get you home and in bed."

"I can't get any sicker."

"Yes, you can. An infection in your lungs would be terrible. I won't have you getting pneumonia, if I can help it."

"Thanks, Mom."

With a quick turn of the head, her mom smiled, then faced the road again.

A warm bed and a good night's sleep sounded wonderful. Maybe if she was lucky, there'd be more kisses from Ryder.

Chapter 12

After being kissed at least a hundred times last night, Amber was in an exceptionally good mood. "Another one?" She nodded to the box her mom set on the dresser.

"Yep."

"More books?"

"No. *Photos*."

Amber scooted up in her bed. "Of who?"

"Oh ... Me. Your grandparents. You as a baby. Lots of people."

"Dad?" Amber scrunched her eyes shut, waiting for the repercussions. The silence that followed made her open one eye for a peek.

Her mom dug around in the box as if hunting for treasure. "A few." She glanced over her shoulder. "But don't get too excited."

How could she get excited about a man she didn't remember? He'd left before she lost her first tooth.

With a handful of photos, her mom sat on the edge of the bed. Amber scooted over to make more room for her.

"Here you are on Santa's lap." Her mom passed the picture. "You were only four."

Seeing herself in a red and green frilly dress made Amber giggle. "I was cute. But ... was I crying?"

"Yep. You were scared of him at first. Then your dad—"

"My *dad?*"

Her mom took the photo from her and stared at it. "He ... He promised you ice cream if you'd smile for the camera. Then he kissed you on the forehead and backed away." She wiped her eyes quickly; almost like she'd tried to hide the fact the memory caused tears. "You smiled for him *and* for Santa Claus."

Amber's fondness for sweets went *way* back. "Did I get ice cream?"

"Of course." She shuffled the photo under the others. "One of the only times he kept his word." Instant bitterness. She shook her head—obviously trying to rid herself of the memories of *him*—then handed her another picture. "Your grandma. I think she was seventeen in this one. You look a lot like her."

Though a black and white photo, Amber could definitely see a likeness. "We have the same nose."

"Yes, you do. Mom had the blondest hair when she was young. I always wished I had her hair, but got Dad's dark hair instead. I passed it on to you."

"And now I look like grandpa did before he died." Amber rubbed her smooth dome.

Her mom responded with a roll of her eyes, then pointed to another photo. "Look at this one." Her eyes lit up. She acted oddly *happy.* "Mom's hair was so curly!"

Amber managed to grasp it, then pulled it closer. Something seemed familiar about it. "How old was she?"

"Oh, I don't know. Barely over two. She was a pudgy little girl."

"Cute." Amber grinned, hoping to encourage her mom's improved mood. "*Cute* is acceptable when referring to kids and puppies."

"Thanks for the clarification." A returned grin affirmed Amber had done the right thing. "I always wanted a puppy." Her mom's shoulders slumped, and she sighed.

"You did? I thought you hated dogs."

"No. I *made* myself hate them because Mom wouldn't let me have one."

"Why? I didn't think Grandma was that kind of person."

"Your grandma was a wonderful mother. Always tried to do what was best for me. But, she saw her dog get run over when she was young. It broke her heart. She didn't want me to have to go through losing something I loved." The sadness in her eyes tugged at Amber's heart.

Amber patted her mom on the hand to get her attention. "Sounds like someone I know."

"What do you mean? I let you have a *cat* when you were little."

"I'm not talking about pets. You think it's good I won't ever fall in love because then I won't be hurt. Right?"

"Yes."

"So what's the difference? Your mom denied you a dog because she was hurt when hers died. Why keep something from *you* because *she* was afraid?"

Blank stare.

Maybe I'm making sense.

Her mom resumed digging in the box. "Wow. Look at this one, Amber."

Amber's hand trembled more than normal when she took the photo. "Playland Pier." Simply saying it wrenched her heart.

"Baby? Are you okay? You're so pale—and you're shaking." Her mom tried to take it, but Amber clutched it as tightly as she could.

"The Ferris wheel." Amber closed her eyes and recalled it vividly. The scent of cotton candy mixed with Ryder's cologne. The red-cushioned seat that swayed in the warm air. The feel of his lips covering hers.

Love.

Her mom stood and returned the rest of the photos to the box, then came back to her side. "Lay back and rest." She placed her hand to Amber's forehead. "You're warm." Again, she tried to take the picture.

"No. I want it."

"You can keep it, but let me put it on the dresser."

"No. I wanna hold it." Amber pressed it close to her heart.

"Why?"

She gulped. "It reminds me of *him*."

"Who?"

"Ryder." She turned her head, unable to take her mom's ugly frown.

"The boy in your dreams? Really Amber? You've got to stop thinking of him like he's a real person. He's not. And what does Playland Pier have to do with him anyway?"

What could it hurt to tell her? She already thought she'd gone crazy, so it didn't matter. Besides, her mom needed to know about *real* love. "He kissed me there. We were on the Ferris wheel. Got stuck at the top, and he kissed me."

Arms folded across chest. *Typical.* "He kissed you. Fine. What harm can there be? No more than you endured from that imaginary friend you had when you were six." Sarcastic. *Totally snarky.*

"Why are you mad? You should be happy I have something good in my life."

"*Happy*? Why be happy about someone who's not real?"

"But he *is* real. He has dark hair. Brown eyes. He's six feet tall. He was born in Colorado and moved here when he was eleven." She glared at her mom. "He has an amazing tattoo on his right arm. And he's a *great* kisser."

"No." She shook her head and backed away. "You've *never* been kissed. And if you ever even *touch* a boy with a tattoo, it would be a mistake. Now, stop pretending and face the truth."

I won't cry. "You're wrong! My dreams are better than my life! He's the best thing that's ever happened to me!"

"Not. Real." With her arrogant chin in the air and her stupid scowl, her mom walked out.

"Yes he is!"

Her mom had always been so eager to take care of her. At least, the *physical* side of her. Why couldn't she see that she only wanted to feel loved? Why be so scared of it?

Amber held up the photo and traced the Ferris wheel with her fingertip. "I know you're real." Tears trickled down her face and puddled in her ears. She closed her eyes.

Please let me sleep.

* * *

Amber's skin warmed from the sun. It covered her like a blanket.

Where am I?

She opened her eyes slowly, then quickly shut them again. The blinding sun beamed directly overhead.

Gulls cried out above her, and she shifted her body. She lay flat on her back on some kind of hard surface wearing the now-familiar white swimsuit.

I need a pillow.

"You sleeping?"

"Huh?" She peered up through squinted eyes, then sighed with contentment.

Ryder ...

"You need more sunscreen." The squirt of a bottle made her giggle, but then she gasped when he touched her. "You don't mind, do you?"

"No. Thank you." Sunscreen wouldn't keep her from melting all over the—wherever it was she was lying. The second his hand touched her skin, she shivered.

He started at her feet and worked up to her thigh. She swallowed hard. Though she needed to, she could barely keep from shaking out of control.

I don't want him to stop.

She blew out a long breath.

His hands quit moving, but remained on her body. "You okay?"

She looked at him and was met with a grin.

You know you're torturing me, don't you?

"Yeah," she muttered. "I'm fine. You?"

"Awesome."

Yes, you are.

Another squirt of the bottle. She jumped when the cold cream landed just above her belly button.

"Too cold?" he asked and smeared it around.

"A little. But I'm not complaining."

She'd never been touched so intimately. He massaged the lotion into her skin, and like the decent guy she assumed him to be, avoided her boobs. Didn't come even *close* to her bikini top.

He moved on to her arms. "Why don't you sit up so I can do your back?"

"Okay."

My back. My front. Anywhere you want.

She eased into a seated position and fully opened her eyes. "No!" She braced her hands against the hard surface. "Get me off this thing!"

Ryder held onto her from behind. "Shh … You're with me. You're safe."

"No!" Surrounded by water, she couldn't breathe. The hard surface she'd been lying on was the white fiberglass of a sailboat.

"Amber. We're on a boat. We're safe. It's no different than the boardwalk."

She pinched her eyes shut. "Yes, it is! I want off."

"You *can't* get off. We're too far from the shore. Focus on me." He turned her in his arms and looked her in the eye. "I won't let anything bad happen to you."

"How'd we get out here?" With slow, deep breaths, she started to calm. But she still wanted off.

"We climbed aboard from the dock. Don't you remember?"

"Uh-uh. You know I hate the water."

He ran his hand through her hair. "Then forget about it." His hands moved around to her back. He drew her in close and kissed her.

My favorite thing.

She grabbed onto him, and every bit of fear melted away. Their lips moved together like old friends. The warmth of his bare skin sent her heart soaring. She glided her hands down his arms in a loving caress. Touching him totally calmed her.

"You're real," she mumbled.

"Of course I am." He stretched out onto his back and pulled her against him. "Now, this isn't so bad, is it?"

Tentatively, she rested her hand on his bare chest. Her head nestled into his shoulder. "No. Just don't let go of me."

"I won't." He stroked her hair. "Ever."

The need to look in his eyes made her rise up on one elbow. His gorgeous face was always worth seeing, but his eyes would tell her the truth. "Promise?"

He touched the tip of her nose. "Promise."

With a sigh, she lay back down. Under any other circumstance, she'd be self-conscious in a bikini. But she wasn't ashamed with him. Everything about him felt as comfortable as breathing. And now that she *could* breathe, she'd enjoy their time together.

She liked resting on his firm chest, but she lifted her head just a little to get a better view of his entire body. Her heart thumped hard. It couldn't take much more. But at least his swim trunks covered his equipment.

Not ready for that.

She traced her finger around his tattoo.

"Why haven't you ever asked me about it?" he whispered.

"Well—I thought you'd just tell me. I mean ..." She rose up again on one elbow. "You don't seem like the tattoo kind of guy."

"Really? What's that mean?" At least he chuckled. She'd not offended him. *Hopefully.*

"My mom always said that guys with tattoos were trouble-makers. But any guy who wears English Leather couldn't cause trouble if he tried." She bit her lower lip, then grinned and looked him in the eye. "You're a *gentleman.* Just like my grandpa was."

"Thank you. I'm glad you gave me a chance."

"So, what's it mean?" She touched the imprinted flower on his bicep. "All these random images."

He pulled her tight against him and blew out a slow breath. She nestled into his body and waited.

"My mom ..." He cleared his throat. His hands glided through Amber's hair. "She died a few years after we moved here."

Amber gasped and clutched him tighter. "I'm so sorry."

"Me, too." He kissed the top of her head. "I took it hard. Made life miserable for my dad. As if he didn't have it hard enough losing her. She was everything to us." His chest rose and fell with every deep breath. "It took me more than a year to stop feeling sorry for myself. Then one day, I looked at my little sister and realized she needed me. Dad did, too."

"You're lucky to have a sister."

"Yep. She's pretty cool."

"So, the tattoo?"

"Every symbol is something my mom liked. The flower's a geranium. Her favorite. And as close as I've seen you study it, I'm sure you've noticed the butterfly, seashell, and musical notes." He pointed to the very top of the design. "Those are angel wings."

If Amber's mom could hear him right now, she'd have second thoughts about tattoos. Amber had never heard anything so beautiful. So much love displayed and cherished. "You're incredible."

They lay quietly for some time. She'd assumed he had the perfect life. Great parents that loved him and were there for him. But he'd felt loss, too.

She wanted to know even more about him. "You're an athlete, aren't you?" He had the most muscular legs she'd ever seen.

"Maybe."

"Don't tease me. What do you play? Soccer? Football?"

"I used to play basketball."

"Makes sense. Your height and all."

Now braver, she thoroughly massaged his smooth tanned chest. A few dark hairs tickled her fingers.

He moaned. "You're killing me, Amber."

"That's the last thing I wanna do."

He flipped her onto her back. "Then kiss me." He bent down, and their bodies entwined. Legs. Arms. *Everything.* With each kiss, their passion intensified.

More …

He wrenched free from her and jumped to his feet. "We gotta stop." Before she even blinked, he leapt over the side of the boat.

"Ryder?" She held her hand to her chest. Her heart beat out of control. She didn't *want* to stop. Why should they? It was only kissing. They'd been doing it a lot lately.

Though she hated to, she inched closer to the edge and peered over the side. No sign of him anywhere. "Ryder!"

Like a cork, he popped to the surface and tossed water from his hair. "What?"

"Don't scare me like that!" The thought of losing him overshadowed every other fear.

"Hey, *I'm* not afraid of the water. I know how to swim."

"I don't care." She swallowed hard. Her heart had finally slowed. "You scared me."

"Sorry." He swam to a ladder hooked to the side of the boat and climbed up. Glistening water dripped from his skin. "I needed to cool off."

"Why?"

"As you would say—*yeah, right.*"

"Don't tease me."

"I'm not. Don't you know what you were doing to me?"

She shrugged and licked her lips. "We were kissing. That's all."

He grabbed a towel and wrapped it around his waist. "Kissing. Yeah. Very *hot* kisses."

Hot? Wow.

She never thought anything she did could be *hot.* "So ... you liked it?"

He eliminated every bit of space between them and wrapped his arms around her. "More than I should. We need to wait."

"For?"

"I know you're not that naïve."

"Oh. You mean. *Sex.*"

"Exactly."

Is he blushing?

She bit her lower lip. "I thought all guys wanted it."

"We do. But that doesn't give me the right to just take it."

He should give Leech Lips some lessons.

She ran her fingers into his hair. "You're something special, you know it?"

"Why do you say that?"

"Because you really care about me. You're not just out to get something."

He cupped her hands inside his, then raised them to his lips and kissed them. "I don't just *care* about you." His eyes burned into her. Set her on fire. "I *love* you."

She teetered and laid her head against him. "Say it again."

"I love you, Amber."

The words she never thought she'd hear. She wanted to cry, and for once, it had nothing to do with pain. She slowly turned her head and kissed the center of his chest, then looked up into his eyes. "I love you, too."

The kiss that followed rivaled all others. Warm and tender, but full of sparks.

We're in love.

If only she could freeze the moment and make it last forever. It no longer mattered that they drifted in the middle of the lake on a boat. Ryder had her floating on air.

She closed her eyes and concentrated on his hands on her skin.

He caressed her back and gave her shivers. "Amber?"

Breathing hard, she looked up at him. "Yeah?"

"Do you trust me?"

"Completely."

He studied her face, then took her hand and moved toward the ladder. "Come with me into the water."

"Uh-uh." *Why?* She tried to back away, but he wouldn't let go.

"You can't get hurt here. Don't you know that?"

She trusted *him*, but *water* ... "I'm scared."

"I know. I swear, once you get in, you'll see there's nothing to fear." He took a step down and pulled her closer. "Focus on the ladder, not the water."

She wanted more than anything to prove she believed in him.

Don't be afraid.

She stepped onto the top rung. Her knuckles turned white, gripping the handrail.

He let go of the ladder and treaded water below her. "Good girl. Keep coming."

She took another step down. Water splashed against her bare feet. And just like it had when they'd waded, it felt more like bath water than lake water. *Warm.* The perfect temperature.

"You're doing awesome, Amber. Just two more steps."

Two more steps, and I'll go under.

The deck of the boat called out to her. She took a single step *up* the ladder. "I need a life jacket."

"No you don't. Just keep coming."

The fear of a five-year-old girl barely breathing on the beach rushed over her. "I can't do it."

"I'm here for you. Now, step *down* again. Take those last steps."

Why am I afraid? Death's been a part of my life for years.

She didn't *step*.

She let go.

Warmth surrounded her.

"I knew you could do it." Ryder's arms encircled her. The water was almost up to their necks, but it was more like being in a bowl of clear Jell-O. Not totally liquid. It held them up, even without moving their legs.

"Am I *swimming*?" She skimmed her hand through the substance.

"Sort of." He laughed and pushed a piece of hair out of her face. "I should've known something like this would happen. You're pretty incredible."

She tipped her head back, and her entire body popped to the surface. The weird water kept her atop it. She floated, completely at ease. "I like this." She shut her eyes and drifted.

"Knew you would. Sometimes you just have to let go." He swam to her and placed a hand on her belly. "I'm glad you trusted me."

"I'll *always* trust you. I love you ..."

"I hope you can eat."

"Huh?"

"I said I hope you can eat."

"Mom?"

Amber's bed felt harder than ever.

CHAPTER 13

With Ryder in her life, Amber stopped feeling sorry for herself. For the most part. Her improved attitude helped the relationship with her mom. They talked more. Of course, Amber couldn't say a word about Ryder or it would ruin her good mood.

The other instant mood-changer occurred whenever she brought up her dad. Anytime Amber asked what had happened to him, she clammed up. *Bitterly.*

But no matter how *happy* Amber let on to be, death drew closer. Weak and light-headed, she had no choice but to use the metal walker. She hated it, but it was better than the alternative.

When I die, I'll lose Ryder.

She had to quickly dismiss the thought. She'd become more worried about losing him than she feared dying. She'd been preparing to die for years now, but the short time she had left wouldn't be nearly enough with him.

She'd make the best of every day *and* every night. Naps were pretty awesome. The long hours of sleep each night spent with Ryder were even better.

They still kissed—*a lot*—but it always stopped there. She tried to stay content, but finally understood desire. She had an aching need to crawl inside him and get lost forever. At times she wished he wasn't so proper. Curiosity and longing sparked a need to go further.

She loved him and wanted to know what it felt like to *make* love before she died.

* * *

Up and down. Slow and smooth. Amber shut her eyes tight and enjoyed the sensation.

"Do you wish it was faster?" Ryder's hand rested in the center of her back.

"No, I like it like this." She leaned backward and let her hair cascade over his hand. "It's the perfect speed."

"You're so adorable. You look like a little girl." He laughed so loud that the sound overpowered the music from the carousel.

"Me?" She opened her eyes and gave him a sideways look. "You're the one I had to coax onto this thing. I didn't know someone your age could pout like a little boy."

"I didn't *pout*. I just prefer the Ferris wheel, that's all."

She nearly had to drag him onto the carousel. When she'd finally talked him into it, he'd chosen a stationary horse. No fun at all, but he'd picked it anyway.

She took hold of the plastic reins and spun them in the air. "Woo-hoo!"

"You're crazy, Amber."

She cocked her head, then flashed her most sultry smile. "Crazy for you."

He hopped off his immobile beast and grabbed her around the waist. Not an easy thing to do since she steadily moved up and down. He stood on his toes to kiss her, but by the time his lips came close to hers, she'd reached eye level.

"Better do it quick!" She giggled.

They'd come to Playland Pier many times, and this was the first time she'd convinced him to ride the carousel.

"Come here," he said and lifted her off the horse. He leaned her against the unmoving one and kissed her thoroughly.

She stroked his face and stared into his dark eyes. "I think I've lost count of our kisses."

"You've been counting?"

"At first."

"Oh. So now I'm just old hat?" He kept his arms around her locked tight.

"You use some of the weirdest expressions. But no matter what you mean, nothing about your kisses will ever get old."

"So." He gave her a peck on the tip of her nose. "Now that you drug me on this thing, it's time you get on the one ride *I've* wanted to go on since the first time we came here."

Instant panic. She frantically shook her head. "Uh-uh. I'll watch you ride, but no way am I getting on those swings."

"But you're not afraid of the water anymore."

"No, but ..."

"So you have no excuse."

The carousel crept to a stop. Their bodies lurched together as it came completely to rest.

He grabbed her hand. "C'mon. It'll be fun."

There's nothing to be afraid of ... There's nothing to be afraid of ...

Maybe if she thought it over and over again, she'd believe it.

Now Ryder looked even more like a little boy. But this time he appeared to be the *happy* little guy about to get his dearest wish. He beamed brighter than the water glittering in the background. The incredibly *deep* water.

He helped her into her swing, then dropped the metal bar in front of her.

No ride attendant?

She gazed upward at the long span of chain links.

I'm gonna be sick.

Ryder sat in the one next to her then grabbed hold of her chain. "I'll hold onto you when the ride starts, but then I'll let go."

"You don't have to." *Please don't let go.*

"Of course, I do. It's more fun when you're flying freely."

Flying freely?

She covered her face with her hands.

"Don't worry, Amber. You're gonna love this."

Right on cue, the swings moved. First they rose higher off the ground, then the machine started to rotate in a circle.

Her stomach turned a flip. Or maybe it'd actually stayed behind somewhere below. Whatever the case, the momentum of the ride picked up.

"Open your eyes, Amber!" Ryder released her chain. "It's like flying!"

She didn't want to. All she could visualize were the chains breaking and her body hurled out into the water.

"C'mon, Amber! This is awesome!" Ryder's enthusiasm didn't help.

Why'd I let him talk me into this?

Gradually, she opened one eye and was dumb enough to look down. She soared high above the water.

She let out a scream, but then started to laugh and opened both eyes wide. The sensation overwhelmed her. Feeling lighter than air, she glided through the warmth of a perfect afternoon. The swing soared round and round, inward and outward. Her feet dangled freely.

Some distance away, Ryder whooped and laughed. Full of life and joy. Her heart leapt. She didn't want it to end.

And now that she felt completely at ease, just like everything else, the ride slowed and came to a stop.

Ryder hopped from his seat, then helped her. Once they were clear of the ride, he lifted her off the ground and swung her around. "I'm so proud of you!"

"That was awesome!" She giggled and hung on tight to his neck. "Not sure why I was afraid."

"I told you you'd like it." He kissed her forehead. "Want to go again?"

She caught sight of the fortune-telling machine over his shoulder. Odd, because she didn't recall it being in that particular spot.

"Maybe in a minute. But first I think you need to get your fortune told. You've never done it. Got a penny?"

"Sure." He dug into his pocket and pulled out a shiny one.

"Cool. Let's go see what the old gypsy has to say. Either that or we can go ride the carousel again before we do the swings a second time."

He shook his head. "Gypsy."

"Okay. We can do the rides again later."

He started to hand her the penny, but she stopped him. "Remember? You said the person getting their fortune told has to put it in. So *you* do it."

"Oh. That's right." He dropped the coin into the slot.

And just like before, the figure inside the glass case moved with creaks and groans.

"They really need to oil this thing," Amber said.

A white card popped out and fluttered to the ground. Ryder bent down and picked it up.

His face hardened, and he frowned as he silently read.

"What?" Amber reached for it.

"It's nothing." He shrugged it off and went to toss it in a trashcan.

Amber grabbed it and read it before he could. "Hmm. Never be afraid to run? Weird. That's not much of a fortune."

"Pretty lame if you ask me."

She stepped away from him. "You're upset. I can tell."

"No, I'm not."

"Yes, you are."

He let out a long breath, then drew her close. "It's nothing." His hand wove through her hair. "Let's go ride some more. How about something totally different? Bumper cars maybe?"

She rested her head on his chest. His heart thumped hard against her cheek. "Sure. But just hold me for a few minutes first, k?"

In all their time together, there'd been only a few moments like this. Somehow, she knew he needed to be held, but he'd never admit it. Easier for her to just make him think *she* needed comfort. He'd always been so eager to help her overcome her fears, but something troubled *him*. There'd been too many times his mood had unexplainably changed. Maybe one day she'd know. Hopefully soon.

* * *

Christmas would arrive in three days. Until a hospice nurse showed up, Amber knew she had *some* time left. From everything she understood about what would happen, the nurse would come in for her final weeks. But, by that time, she'd probably be oblivious to everything.

Please let me live a little longer.

Her mom bounded into the room waving a pamphlet. "I have a great idea!"

"Disneyland?"

Her mom scowled. "No. Something closer to home."

Of course. Amber was too weak to travel so far. "Walmart?"

"*Funny.*" She carefully handed her the brochure. Her pained expression while she watched Amber's hands shake almost ruined the joy of the moment. "Unless you don't want to go on a boat."

The tension in her mom's face relaxed when Amber steadied the pamphlet and opened it. She had to concentrate hard, but managed to completely relax her trembling fingers. She smiled. "I'm good with boats. This looks like fun." Since she'd had some of her finest kisses with Ryder on many of them, she and boats had become best friends.

She decided to read the brochure aloud. "Take this magical journey to see one and a half million lights. Visit the North Pole and meet Santa and his elves." She glanced at her mom. "Maybe I won't cry this time." They both grinned. "But seriously, do you think I'm up to it?"

"You'll have to stay in a wheelchair. Bundled up, of course. But I think you need to get out and do something fun. You game?"

"Can Stephanie go with us?"

"I suppose. But what if she wants to bring her boyfriend?"

"Will you help me throw him overboard?"

Her mom covered her mouth and laughed. "Shame on you, Amber."

Amber laughed right along with her. Because of the exceptional mood in the room, she decided to push her luck. "Mom?"

"Yes?" Her laughter continued while she sat down.

"I'm not afraid of water anymore. Ryder helped me get over it."

Instant ice. "Don't start, Amber. I thought you were over all that."

"Okay. I won't talk about *him*."

Ask her.

Amber took a quick breath. "I don't want you to leave my room until you tell me about Dad." She spit it all out so fast, she surprised herself. "Why'd he leave?"

Rigidly, her mom stood. "No. We're through here." She headed for the door.

"No we're not! Don't walk out on me, Mom. You're acting just like Dad!"

She whipped around and in two strides stood beside her. "Don't *ever* say that!" Her hand flew into the air, then stopped and hovered over Amber's head, shaking out of control.

Amber cowered.

Her mom crumpled back into the chair. "God, I don't know what I'm doing anymore." She placed her head in her hands and leaned forward into her lap. She rocked back and forth.

Amber swallowed hard and pushed on. "I wanna know."

"No you don't."

"Yes I do."

Her mom's head lifted. She glared with eyes sharp as razor blades. "Not telling you protects you. Understand?"

Amber shook her head and focused on the ceiling. "I'm dying. Why do I need to be protected? I mean—was he some kind of spy? Will assassins come after me because I learned the truth?" Yes, she'd been sarcastic, but her mom was being ridiculous.

"Always so smart. Aren't you?"

"Tell me, and I'll never bring it up again."

Her mom sat up and leaned back in the chair. Her face froze as hard as stone—tight-lipped. No smile. No frown. Her chest heaved up and down, and every breath she took hissed from her nose. "Fine. But I warned you." She pointed her index finger like a knife.

Amber folded her arms across her chest and matched her coldness. She could be just as defiant and stubborn. "I'm listening."

"So, you're not afraid of the water anymore? Hmm?"

"Nope." *I'm not afraid of anything.*

"And you remember almost drowning, though you were only five?"

"It's my first memory. Hard to forget something like that."

Her mom leaned in, icy as ever. "Do you remember who you were with when it happened?"

"No."

With a grunt, her mom stood, crossed to the window, and faced the street.

What's she looking at?

She braced her hand on the wall and drummed her fingers. "You were with *him*. Your dad."

"I was?"

Her head bobbed. "Summer on the beach. Our favorite time of year. I was at work that day." She huffed. "I'll never forget it. He called me and told me he'd gotten into an argument with his boss. It wasn't time for him to leave, but he said he was going home." She let out a small groan. "Said he might even quit."

Amber's chest tightened. She didn't like where this was heading.

"He took you out of daycare." She moved away from the window and looked directly at her. "You didn't want to go with him, because you were having fun playing with the other kids. They told me you screamed as he carried you out the door. That you were crying. Begging to stay."

The tension in Amber's chest turned instantly to tears.

"Before hitting the beach, your dad bought a six pack, then headed for a nice sandy spot. Probably got an eyeful watching women in bikinis." Another grunt. "He drank one beer right after another. Forgot you were playing in the water."

"Did he get drunk?"

"Drunk enough. Didn't even realize you'd gone under. Someone else pulled you from the water. Gave you mouth-to-mouth." Her mom stared blankly. "He didn't have a clue until he heard the commotion. Even then, he was so numb from drinking, it didn't sink in. I got a call from a police officer. They took you both to the hospital."

"What did Dad say when you got there?"

"He blubbered like a baby. Told me he was sorry. And I told him he was a *shit* and had no business being a father."

Amber wiped her eyes. "And he left?"

"Two days later."

"But—"

"But nothing, Amber. He only cared about himself. Not you *or* me. I didn't regret one word I said to him." Her face drew tight with anger. "The night he left, he said I was right. Said you deserved a better dad. He grabbed a bottle of beer from the refrigerator and went out the door."

"He left because of me?"

"Why do you think I didn't want to tell you?"

Amber took deep breaths to control the pain in her heart. It constricted and weighed her down. She sunk deeper into the pillows. "But I didn't die. I mean—he didn't have to leave."

"What?" Her mom's eyes popped wide and filled with fire. "How can you say that? He drank until he was so out of it he forgot he *had* a daughter!"

"He was upset. His job and all—"

"Stop! Don't you *dare* defend him. He told me he was sorry, and two days later, he left!"

"Why didn't you stop him? If he knew he was wrong you could've helped him through it. Got him in AA or something. When you love someone you're supposed to help them!"

Her mom let out a weird little laugh. She shook her head and looked at her as if she'd turned into someone she didn't recognize. "You're so naïve, Amber. You don't know anything about love."

"Yes, I do! Ryder's shown me more love than you *ever* have!"

"Stop it! I swear ... if you ever say his name again I'll ..."

"What? What will you do to me?"

Her mom glared, breathing hard. "You wanted to hear the truth about your dad. I told you. He walked out on us and never looked back. But now it's my turn. I want you to stop living in your dreams and prepare for what's coming."

Amber didn't utter a sound.

"I'm tired of arguing." Her mom let out an exasperated sigh. "If we're facing this head-on—as you said you wanted to—then let's stop fighting and try to get along. Please?"

Amber hated fighting. It made her sicker than she already was.

I just won't talk about Ryder anymore. I'll keep him to myself.

"I'll try." Amber fidgeted with the blanket. "But ... Can I ask you one more question?"

"What?"

"How were you able to divorce Dad?"

"I didn't."

"Oh." Amber always assumed they had.

"We've been better off without him." She walked out of the room.

Amber let her tears fall, feeling a new kind of pain. She thought about her photo with Santa Claus and how her dad had made her smile.

I know he loved me.

But how could a man who loved her walk away and never give her another thought? If he'd fallen out of love with her mom, he could've just divorced her. Then at least Amber would've known him—made memories with him. He would've been a part of her life. She had lots of friends whose parents were divorced. Somehow they'd made it work.

If I wasn't so sick, I'd try to find him.

She had no recollection of any family on his side. Her mom had told her a long time ago that her Grandma and Grandpa Stewart had died before she was born. But there had to be other relatives that might know where he'd gone.

I can't ask Mom.

Amber had promised she'd let it drop. But knowing all this only added more questions.

I guess I'll never know.

CHAPTER 14

"Just hold me." Amber nestled into Ryder's arms. This time *she* needed *him*. Needed to be comforted.

Safe.

Warm.

Loved.

He kissed the top of her head. "Gladly."

The city park seemed extra quiet today. If not for the bird chirping in the branch above them, their breathing would be the only sound. Both dressed in their usual comfortable jeans, Ryder had on one of his sexy tanks that showed off his muscles and made her heart patter a little faster. She doubted her simple pink t-shirt had the same effect on him.

They snuggled together on a soft blanket. He leaned against a thick-trunked tree, and she cuddled against him. She burrowed into his body like he'd turned into the world's finest pillow. If only she could stay here forever.

She'd hoped being with him would wash away all the memories of the horrible fight with her mom. But, even in this dream world, real life had managed to hang around her shoulders like a lead weight.

She nuzzled closer to him.

Maybe he sensed her stress, because he instantly started rubbing her back.

"Mmm ..." she murmured. "That's nice."

"I'll let you return the favor later."

"No problem." She looked up into his eyes and smiled. "But you keep that up, and I might fall asleep."

"No. There's none of that here." He bent down and kissed her. It took away all thoughts of sleeping.

What would happen if I slept in a dream?

The fact she knew she was in a dream troubled her enough.

She sat fully upright. "There's that little girl again. And she's chasing the same puppy."

With her kinky blonde curls bouncing, the chubby-legged girl passed by them, giggling. "Puppy!" She followed the dog—always just out of reach.

Her mom trailed right behind her. "Anna, slow down. I don't want you to fall."

The pretty woman stopped within ten feet of them. She looked sideways and met Amber's gaze. "Someday you'll see. Children are such a joy."

And then, like a mist, she disappeared along with the child and puppy.

"Strange," Ryder said. "But honestly, nothing surprises me when I'm with you."

She giggled and relaxed against him.

He lovingly rubbed her arm. "That woman got me thinking."

"Uh-oh. We're in trouble now." She peered up at him and batted her eyes, which prompted him to lean down and give her another incredible kiss.

She mindlessly stroked his chest. "I'll never get enough of your kisses." To prove herself, she lifted up and kissed him again. "So, what did she make you think about?"

"Kids."

"Yeah?"

"I'd like to have a few. *Someday.*" His fingers slid through her hair. "And this should come as no surprise, but I'd like to have them with *you.*"

She sat up and leaned away from him. "Can we?"

His brows rose. "I'm pretty sure we can figure out how."

"*Funny.* But—"

"But what? Amber, anything's possible here."

Her mind spun.

Anything's possible?

She stood and gazed around the park. So perfectly beautiful and peaceful. She'd grown to accept it as a part of her life. Her life with Ryder. But the idea of kids hadn't crossed her mind as a possibility.

She sensed his presence behind her. He pushed her hair off her neck and glided his lips along her bare skin. Instant shivers.

"We'd have fantastic kids," he said. While he spoke, his lips brushed against her.

Her breath hitched. "I'd want them to look like you." She faced him. His mouth drifted from her neck to her face and touched it with the softest of kisses. Then he moved to her lips and drank her in like water. She clasped onto him, wanting more.

He pulled back, then smiled and put his mouth to her ear. "I'd have to marry you first."

"To have kids?"

"Yes, what else did you think I meant?"

"Sorry. I was just thinking about *other* things." *And it's all your fault.*

"I have those thoughts all the time." He leaned backward and created a V between them. "And ... I'd still need to marry you first."

"Are you some kind of saint?"

He erupted into laughter. "Hardly. Some of my thoughts about you are anything but pure."

"Then why?"

He patted himself on the chest and got one of the goofiest looks she'd seen yet. Then he hooked his thumbs into the straps of his tank top and wiggled his fingers. "I, my dear, am a *gentleman*. Or, did you forget? You said it yourself."

"You're weird."

"You've said that before, too."

She fluttered her lashes. "And how, pray tell, did this gentlemanly way come to pass?" She could play this game. She'd seen enough old movies to come up with a corny line.

His demeanor changed, and he became Ryder again, lighting up with an incredible smile.

Thank God.

"My dad showed me how to be a gentleman," he said. "He treated my mom with amazing respect. Set a good example."

"You're lucky." *Man was he ever.* She'd never tell him about *her* dad.

"Yes, I am. Especially with you in my life."

"You always do that." She swatted him playfully on the chest.

"What?" He rubbed the spot like she'd hurt him. Complete with a protruding lip.

"Say nice things about me." She set his lip right again with a decent kiss.

"I haven't found anything about you I don't like. Except maybe your feet."

"You!" She grabbed hold of him and wrestled him to the ground.

They laughed and tumbled together onto the blanket, then stifled each other with long heated kisses.

But then, a much wetter tongue joined in.

Amber pushed away when the long puppy tongue slurped across her face. "Hey!"

Ryder sat back on his heels. He laughed even harder.

"Go on and laugh," she said. She grabbed the dog and held it far away from her. It continued to squirm, and its tongue lapped in midair. "How is it I'm the one who got all the puppy slobber?"

"Puppy!"

The little girl had returned. She toddled over to them dressed in a cute frilly sundress and ruffled bloomers. Her hands reached out, and she wiggled her tiny fingers.

"You've been chasing him a long time," Amber said. "Why don't you sit down here on the blanket, and you can hold him?"

The girl giggled and plopped down right beside her. Again, she held out her hands.

Though a puppy, the dog probably weighed at least ten pounds. A not-so-little chocolate Labrador. She carefully set him on the girl's lap.

He wiggled and squirmed and licked the girl all over, prompting more giggles.

"Anna?" The girl's mom had also come back. "Are you bothering these nice people?"

"No, Mommy." With extra wide eyes, Anna tilted her head.

Amber looked over at Ryder, who grinned from ear-to-ear.

He really does like kids.

Of course, this particular kid happened to be adorable.

Hard not to like her.

Anna struggled with the dog. Not surprising since it was almost as big as her.

Ryder picked up a long stick. The thing had a few leaves on one end. "Anna? Why don't we go over there and play fetch with the dog?" He nodded to a large span of treeless grass.

She laughed and clapped her hands.

The puppy jumped from her lap and romped over to Ryder. The second Ryder got on his feet, the little pup yipped and wagged its tail. It followed him, leaping for the stick in Ryder's hand.

Ryder lobbed it a short distance. The dog bolted, and Anna tottered after him. Her mom let out a sweet, rich laugh. Probably the most sophisticated female laughter Amber had ever heard.

"Anna," the woman said. "Don't fall."

Amber assumed that if the girl fell, she wouldn't get hurt. She'd most likely bounce off the ground. Maybe even float.

"She's really cute," Amber said to her. "And so happy."

"It's impossible to be *unhappy* here. No one should know that better than the two of you. You've been blessed."

She'd made a good point. Every bit of stress Amber had felt when she got here had disappeared. Happiness consumed her.

Ryder had been busy throwing the stick and playing with Anna, so she doubted he'd heard the remark. His laughter warmed her through and through. The way he tried to show Anna how to throw the stick made him even more amazing. Patient and good. Evidence of the loving person she believed him to be.

The woman had also been watching them play. She held her hands to her chest, and her eyes sparkled. They held no fear, only complete trust.

"Should I know you?" Amber asked.

An enormous smile answered her question.

"I should, shouldn't I?"

"Search your heart, Amber."

She knows my name. Maybe she heard Ryder say it.

Amber blinked, and she vanished.

"Where'd they go?" Ryder ran over to her, holding the stick. He looked totally confused and a little disappointed. Anna and the puppy had also disappeared.

Amber shrugged. "Typical of this place. But as long as *you* don't evaporate, I'll be happy."

"Then, be happy. I'm not going anywhere." His frown went away. He tossed the stick over his shoulder and pulled her down onto the blanket.

"Wait." She stopped him from kissing her. "What about the puppy slobber?"

He chuckled. "Puppy slobber? Guess it vanished, too." He covered her with kisses of his own.

CHAPTER 15

"Okay. Are you sure you'll be warm enough?"

Amber rolled her eyes. Her mom had asked the same question three times already.

"I'll be fine, Mom. We need to go. Stephanie and the jerk are waiting."

"Attitude, Amber." She started the engine.

"Sorry. I just wish he wasn't going. That's all."

Amber stared out the window of their van. Snow lightly fell. Tiny fluffy flakes. Several inches had already covered the ground, and she'd suggested they stay home. But her mom remained determined to get her out to see the Christmas lights.

After their Thanksgiving ordeal, she thought for sure this trip would be canceled. But Dr. Carmichael had adjusted her pain meds, and she didn't feel as nauseated as she'd been then. So they figured they might as well give it a try. Just in case, there were still plenty of barf bags in the glove compartment. Her mom had also crammed a few in her purse. Always prepared.

"Glad I got those new snow tires put on," her mom said. They approached a stop sign, and she carefully pumped the brakes. They squeaked with every push.

"Maybe you should've gotten new brakes instead."

A quick sideways grin from her mom eased the tension in the car. Having her in a good mood made things even better.

"Want to sing Christmas carols?" Her mom asked the question with a much larger grin.

"Uh-uh."

"Ah ... C'mon. Humor me."

"Okay. Just one. But once we pick up Steph and *him,* I don't wanna sing."

I probably won't talk much either.

Her mom drummed her fingers on the steering wheel. "Well? What song should we sing?"

"You suggested singing, so you choose."

"'Silent Night?'"

"Sure. I like that one."

It'd always been a favorite. Ever since she sang a verse by herself at the church Christmas pageant. She'd been eight years old at the time, and her mom thought for sure she'd be the next Rebecca St. James.

They sang out and even harmonized.

"Darn good," her mom said after the final note.

"Yeah, right." Amber had heard more than one clunker note.

"Yeah. *Right.*" She steered the van into the Smiths' driveway. "I'll go get them."

Amber laughed out loud.

Like I could.

"Tell them *Merry Christmas* for me," Amber called out after her.

In only a few moments, her mom returned. Stephanie and Jason trailed behind her. They, too, were bundled for the cold. Heavy coats, scarves, and gloves. Stephanie also wore a cute knit hat. A good-looking couple, but the truth about Jason's real character ruined the pretty picture.

She's way too good for the guy.

After sliding the van door to the side, they climbed into the back seat.

"Hey Amber," Stephanie said. Her smile brightened the interior of the van. "This is gonna be fun."

"Hope so." Amber glanced at Jason. "Have you ever seen the lights across the lake?"

"Nah. But I'm cool with it." He tossed his head, and his hair fell perfectly back into place. If he sat any closer to Stephanie, he'd be on top of her.

Maybe that's the idea.

Amber faced forward. She had to stop thinking bad thoughts about the guy or the night would be completely miserable.

If I don't have fun, Mom will never forgive me.

Mumbling that came from the back seat turned Amber's head. Jason's mouth was so close to Stephanie's ear it might as well have been inside it. The way Stephanie's eyes kept changing shape, she could only imagine what he'd said to her.

Amber decided to interrupt. "Did you know they have a fireworks show, too?"

Stephanie giggled. "I like fireworks."

"I can show you some fireworks, babe," Jason muttered against Stephanie's cheek.

Amber grunted. From now on, she'd keep her eyes glued to the front window.

"We're here!" Her mom chimed like an alarm clock. She wasn't stupid. She'd probably heard what had been going on behind her.

Amber waited patiently while her mom got the wheelchair from the back of the van. Once she'd settled into the chair, her mom stuffed a heavy quilt around her. "Warm enough?" She patted Amber's cheek, then adjusted her headscarf.

"Almost *too* warm."

"Good." She took her place behind her and wheeled her down the ramp to the dock.

Recalling her time on the boardwalk with Ryder, Amber's heart fluttered.

Wish you were here.

Then again, she'd never want him to see her like this. Not that she believed he'd love her any less, but why spoil the perfect image he had of her?

Twinkling lights covered the two-story cruise boat and set the mood for the lights to come.

Sometimes being in a wheelchair had its advantages. They were allowed on the boat before other passengers boarded and didn't have to wait outside in the cold.

Her mom wheeled her to a good spot on the bottom deck. It had a great view. "We'll go to the outside rail when we get to the light display. I don't want you out in that frigid air for long."

"Sounds good to me," Amber said. "I like it in here." She appreciated the warmth and comfort of the enclosed portion of the boat.

"Steph," Jason said. His lecherous arms wrapped around Stephanie's waist. "Let's check out the rest of the boat." He glanced at Amber. "You mind?"

"No." Amber waved him away. "Go now before the boat fills up."

"Cool." He tugged on Stephanie's hand and took her away before the girl had time to do a double-take.

Amber's mom pulled out a chair from a long table and set it beside her. "I don't know about that boy."

"I'm trying not to think about him." Amber gazed out the window. "Just remember what you promised me about

Stephanie. She likes you, Mom. After I'm gone, be sure to check on her now and then. K?"

"I will." She rubbed Amber's back.

The interior of the boat got warmer as more and more passengers came aboard. Tons of kids talked nonstop, carrying on about how excited they were to see Santa Claus.

Every now and then, one would freeze in front of her and stare. Their curiosity didn't make a whole lot of sense. If she'd left her headscarf off it would've been different, but she'd kept her bald head covered specifically for this reason.

Don't wanna freak out the little kids.

If they gaped for too long, Amber would just give them one of her best smiles and they'd leave—usually escorted by a parent who looked horrified, probably afraid their child might say the wrong thing.

When the boat finally left the dock, Amber couldn't have been more ready. Truthfully, she was tired and feared she might fall asleep upright in the wheelchair.

The motion from the choppy water had her stomach churning. She told her mom she felt queasy, so she went to the drink bar and brought back a pop.

"I hope this helps," she said and handed her the drink. Then she patted her purse. "But remember, if you think you might have to throw up ..."

"I know. You have the barf bags."

And wouldn't that be just great. Hurling in front of a bunch of kids.

Amber sipped the bubbling drink. It seemed to help.

Her mom stayed right by her side. Ready to help her if she needed her. Unlike her best friend and the girl's stupid boyfriend.

They were getting closer to the light display at Casco Bay. This time of year they referred to it as the North Pole. The volume from the kids doubled. Amber recalled a time when she would've been right there with them. Excited about Santa, and presents, and everything associated with Christmas. But she could barely keep her eyes opened and her stomach calm.

The sky had almost darkened. She hadn't moved since she'd been parked by the window. "What do you think happened to Stephanie and Jason?"

"Not sure." Her mom sipped on a cup of hot chocolate. "They probably went to the upper deck."

No, more like they found a dark corner somewhere. "Yeah. Probably."

"Amber, don't begrudge Stephanie a boyfriend. It's *possible* we've misjudged him. Stephanie's a sensible girl."

"Ha!" Amber quickly covered her mouth. She hadn't meant for it to come out so loud. About a dozen people whipped their heads around to look at her.

"Mom." She lowered her voice to a whisper. "We aren't wrong about him. You felt it, too. Remember? And you've had lots more experience with guys than I have."

"Yes, I have." Her mouth twisted. "Feel like going outside? Maybe we can find them."

"Sure."

Her mom unlocked the wheels, then grabbed the handles and pushed her through the crowd.

The exterior deck overflowed with people, but somehow they were able to part them easily. Another advantage of being in a wheelchair.

Amber immediately recognized the back of Stephanie's head. Long blonde hair beneath a red knit hat. She and Jason stood at the rail facing the water.

Her eyes were also drawn to something else—the jerk's hand stuffed inside Stephanie's back pocket.

She nodded up at her mom. "See what I mean? I doubt his hands are that cold. Especially in gloves."

She didn't respond, just shook her head. She steered the wheelchair up beside Stephanie.

"Oh," Stephanie said. "I'm glad you came out. We're almost there."

Amber pulled the quilt tighter around her. "We wondered what happened to you." Though warm inside, the cool air out here seeped through her clothes.

"Not like we can go far," Jason said. "And I don't swim." He laughed.

Did he really think that was funny?

Stephanie giggled. "Oh, Jace!" She swatted his arm.

I wish I was home in bed.

The boat slowed, approaching the bay. The sun had completely set. Bright lights from the enormous displays twinkled. Most prominent, a tall Christmas tree that floated on the water.

"Look, Mommy!" a little girl close by yelled and pointed. "Santa Claus!"

The boat swung by the old guy dressed in a Santa suit. He waved and did his best *ho, ho, ho.*

Amber tugged on her mom's coat sleeve. "I promise not to cry." She grinned, and her mom shot her one of her best eye rolls ever.

"Ho! Ho! Ho!" This particular Santa had a lot of energy. "And a merry Christmas to you, Amber Stewart!"

"Huh?" *No way.* "Mom. You set it up, didn't you?"

"My lips are sealed."

Jason sniggered. But before Amber could tell him what she thought of him, fireworks lit up the sky.

Ooh's and *ah's* surrounded them, along with more bursts of multi-colored fireworks.

Caught up in the display, she'd taken her eyes off Stephanie. But when she turned to make a comment to her, found her in a lip-lock with Jason.

C'mon. There are kids here.

So she wasn't supposed to *begrudge* her a boyfriend. Maybe the same applied to their kissing. She should graciously accept their need to play tonsil hockey no matter where they were. After all, she and Ryder had been doing *their* share of kissing.

Nope. Not going to convince myself that what they're doing is anything like what Ryder and I do.

"Mom? Let's go back inside." Amber held her blanket even closer. "I'm kinda cold."

No more had to be said. Her mom whisked her back indoors quicker than she could blink. Stephanie and leech lips were oblivious.

The ride back to the dock went quicker than it had getting to the display. When it came time to leave the boat, Stephanie and Jason appeared miraculously out of nowhere.

They climbed into the back seat while Amber's mom got her settled in the front.

"Did you enjoy it?" she asked and snapped Amber's buckle together.

"Yeah. I did. Thanks."

It seemed to make her mom feel good buckling her seatbelt. Amber assumed Jason thought she'd treated her like a baby, but she didn't care. Doubtful the clueless guy either knew about or *cared* how little she could use her hands anymore. Fastening the seatbelt would've been impossible for her to do on her own.

"I'm glad you had fun," her mom said and kissed her on the cheek. "I did, too." She bustled around to the driver's seat and latched her own belt. "You two buckled up tight back there?"

"Yes, Mrs. Stewart," Stephanie said. "Both of us."

Amber glanced over her shoulder. Once again they were butt-to-butt. She decided to close her eyes and not think about it.

Though just a short ride home, Amber dozed off. Her mom's singing woke her up.

"*We wish you a merry Christmas and a happy New Year!*" She repeated it over and over again. After about the fifth time, she broke out laughing.

What was in her hot chocolate?

No way her mom would drink and drive. More than likely, her behavior came from a nervous-energy sugar high.

When her mom took a large breath like she was about to start another round, Amber had to end it. "Enough already, Mom."

"*Scrooge.*" She gripped the steering wheel with both hands. "You kids warm enough back there?"

"Yes, Mrs. Stewart," Stephanie said.

"Yes, ma'am," Jason added.

Amber braved a quick glance at them, then faced forward and rolled her eyes.

He was *plenty* warm. Especially his hands, which he'd tucked up inside Stephanie's coat.

Don't wanna think about what he's doing with them.

Her mom patted her leg. "Why don't we have some hot chocolate when we get home? Sound good?"

"Sure." She gave the backseat another quick peek.

Making out here?

Because it was so dark in the van, she doubted her mom could see what they were doing in the backseat by looking through the rearview mirror. Amber wished *she* hadn't.

Can't she hear the heavy breathing?

Maybe she just chose to ignore it. It could also explain the unending rendition of "We Wish You a Merry Christmas."

Heaviness weighed down Amber's heart and spirit. The Christmas lights had been great, and the boat ride wasn't half bad. But being incredibly tired, she just wanted to get home and into bed. To go to sleep and be with Ryder again.

Snow had continued to fall throughout the evening and had piled up on the ground. Jason acted like Mr. Perfect and helped her mom with the wheelchair. He even tried to help *her* out of the van and into the chair, but she glared at him. No way would she let him put his hands on her.

"You do it, Mom," Amber said as firmly as she could.

"All right, honey."

Amber put her arm over her mom's shoulder and slid from the seat of the van into her wheelchair. Then her mom pushed her up the sidewalk to the front door. Someone had been nice enough to shovel away the snow, but a thin layer of icy crystals still remained.

"You kids get comfortable on the sofa, and I'll make the cocoa." Her mom positioned the wheelchair in the living room, locked the wheels, and flitted off to the kitchen.

Stephanie took off her coat and sat, then Jason plopped down beside her, frowning. Like he was sorry she'd shed the thing.

Probably wanted to feel her up again.

"No tree?" he asked. His head bobbed around the room.

"No." Amber picked at the armrest on the wheelchair. "Too much trouble."

"No presents?"

She leered at him. "I don't need anything."

He smirked.

Stephanie looped her finger around the chain at her neck. "I almost forgot to show you this. Look what Jason gave me. Isn't it gorgeous?"

"Nice." Amber smiled at her. How could they still be an item after a month and a half?

Sooner or later, it'll get ugly.

She had no doubt.

Jason ran his fingers along the necklace. "I know how to take care of her." His hand brushed across her boob as he pulled it away. "Don't I, babe?"

Did he really think she wouldn't notice? Or maybe he didn't care.

I'm gonna throw up. And her upset stomach had nothing to do with it.

"Uh-huh." Stephanie bit her lip and giggled.

If I wasn't in the room, I bet he'd jump her right there on the couch.

As if he'd known what she'd been thinking, he looked directly at her. "Stephanie hasn't given me *my* present yet. But I'm not asking for much." Again with the stupid smirk.

"Know what *I'd* like to give you?" Amber's blood pressure shot up, and her body trembled. She couldn't catch her breath and gasped for air.

"Amber?" Stephanie stopped smiling. She stood and knelt down in front of her. "Mrs. Stewart!"

Her mom came instantly. "I'm sorry. I need to lay her down. Stephanie, can you call your dad and ask him to come and get you?"

"Sure." She pulled her cell out of her purse. Before calling, she grasped Amber's hand. "Hang in there. K?"

Amber dipped her head.

Why'd I let him get to me?

"Just make yourselves as comfortable as you can until your dad gets here." Her mom waved toward the sofa. "I'm so sorry."

Hopefully they won't get too comfortable.

Her mom wheeled her to her room, then pushed back the covers and helped her undress. "I shouldn't have taken you out tonight."

"No, Mom." She could barely squeak out a weak rasp. "I had fun."

"It was a mistake. I'm so sorry, baby." She lifted her to her feet and guided her into bed.

"Just let me sleep. I'll be fine ..."

A soft kiss to Amber's forehead sent her to sleep. Exactly where she wanted to be.

CHAPTER 16

Amber stood face-to-face with the softest and longest nose she'd ever come so close to.

"Look at you, baby." She stroked the brown fur. "You're beautiful."

The horse puffed out a breath through its nostrils.

"You hungry?" She reached into her pocket and produced a shiny red apple.

The horse bit it in half. One section dropped onto the ground. After chewing up the portion in its mouth, the animal bent down and picked up the rest. Amber laughed when it nudged her pocket, searching for more.

"That's all I have." There were likely more elsewhere. Maybe she could find some.

She took in her surroundings. She'd never been here before.

A long, slatted wood fence surrounded the property, and a thick forest lay beyond it. She stood beside the horse on a plush green pasture. Plenty of room for the animal to run. A large stable with a pretty multi-colored quilt square painted on its pinnacle was on the far side. Another eight horses grazed in the field not far from it.

"You go to your friends." She gave the mare a pat and sent her on her way.

Ryder?

He acted a little dazed standing just outside the fence. As one of the horses trotted by him, he jerked back.

Amber ran to him. "Ryder!" She climbed over the fence and into his arms, but his body was rigid. He didn't even try to hold her. "What's wrong?" She let him go and stepped away.

"I don't know why we're here." No smile. *Cold.*

"But ... this place is beautiful. And the horses are fantastic."

"No. I don't want to be here."

"Why? We could go for a ride."

"No!" He violently shook his head and bolted.

He's so fast.

She'd accused him of being an athlete, and the way he moved proved it.

She flew after him into the woods. With a burst of energy, she grabbed his arm and jerked him to a stop. "What's wrong?"

His damp, sweaty body shook. "I can't."

"Can't what?"

"Go near them." He gestured to the pasture. "I won't."

She placed her hand on his cheek. "You're afraid."

He shut his eyes. "*Terrified.*"

"This coming from the guy who fearlessly swung from trees, jumped off cliffs, and swam in the middle of the lake? Not to mention was brave enough to kiss me in a swinging Ferris wheel seat stuck high up in the air?"

"Yep. Same guy."

Memories of his behavior at the carousel came to mind, but it'd been nothing like this. The poor guy was mortified.

"I didn't think you were afraid of anything," she whispered.

"Wrong."

"But you told me we can't get hurt here." She stroked his face, then ran her hand into his hair, trying to calm him.

"That's right."

"So ..." She nodded her head toward the field.

"No way, Amber."

She placed her hands on her hips. "Ryder. I trusted you enough to get in the water *and* to ride on those swings. Why can't you trust me enough to get on the back of a horse?"

He grabbed her hands and held them in his own. "I never expected *this.*"

He should be used to the unexpected.

"What's so different about *this*? Do you know where we are?"

"My dad's ranch."

"Wow. So, your dad likes horses."

"You could say that."

There had to be more to it. "He sells them? Breeds them?"

"Yep." He turned away.

"And ..." She rubbed his arm.

Finally, he looked directly at her. "He was a pro. A professional cowboy. One of the best."

"That's so cool."

"Yeah. Cool."

"I get it now. Your name." She laughed. "Why didn't you tell me? I mean, c'mon, Ryder. It's obvious they gave you the name for a good reason."

He kicked at the ground with one foot. "It was a curse."

"Now you're being ridiculous."

"No, I'm not. Dad wanted me to follow in his footsteps. My parents used to call me their *little cowboy.*"

"But that's so sweet." His frown indicated his disagreement. "So, what happened?"

"I got thrown when I was ten and was ... *hurt*. After that, I was too scared to get back on and ride."

She took two steps back and studied him.

After she'd been silent for some time, he fanned his arms wide, staring at her. "What?"

"I'm just a little surprised, that's all. Coming from the guy who always tells *me* not to be afraid. I'd say you're overdue."

"No. I'm not riding."

She put her arms around him. "I'll be right beside you on another horse. Nothing bad will happen."

He swallowed so hard his Adam's apple bobbled. "I'm scared."

"I know." She gave him a soft smile, hoping to ease his fears. Their roles had totally reversed. "I can finally do something for *you*. You've helped me more than you'll ever know." She released him and grabbed his hand. "C'mon, Ryder. Let's ride."

She blinked, and they were in the middle of the pasture. Two saddled horses stood beside them.

The brown mare she'd patted earlier nudged her shoulder. "This one's mine," she laughed.

Another mare, black as night, pawed the ground beside Ryder. She raised her head and snorted.

Ryder froze.

Amber crossed to him and framed his face with her hands. "You can do it."

"She looks like the one that threw me."

"Maybe she's giving you a second chance." She handed him the reins. "Put your foot in the stirrup, grab on, and get up there."

He shifted his eyes to look at her, then faced the saddle.

"Go on, little cowboy." Amber patted his butt. "Nice jeans." Truthfully, she liked what was *in* them.

He gave her a quick grin, then hoisted himself onto the horse.

She rushed to her own ride and mounted. With a nudge to its side, the brown took off. Like a shadow, the black followed along.

Amber decided it would be best to stay by Ryder's side for now, so she slowed her horse to let his catch up. "You hanging in there?"

He clutched the horn with both hands. "So far so good."

"Wanna go faster?" She wiggled her brows.

"No."

The way he said it made her laugh. Once again, he looked like a little boy.

So cute.

Don't worry, little cowboy, I'll help you get over your fear.

She lifted her face to the sun. Not a cloud in the sky. Lighter than air, she rode across the pasture to a path in the woods.

The narrow track allowed only a single rider, so she took the lead. She frequently glanced over her shoulder to check on Ryder. At least he'd relaxed. A *little*. He now had only one hand on the horn and actually looked around instead of staring straight ahead like a zombie.

A familiar scent surrounded her, and then she saw them. "Huckleberries!" She jerked the horse to a stop and jumped down.

"What are you doing?"

"Picking huckleberries." She motioned for him to join her. "Come help me."

Carefully, he dismounted.

The bushes overflowed with the plump purple berries. She grabbed them by handfuls. "Mom used to make jam. Oh, and did I tell you my favorite milkshake flavor is huckleberry?"

"No, you never mentioned it." He peered around the woods. "Bears like them, too."

"I know. I saw a mound of purple bear poop one time when we were out picking berries. But I don't think we'll see any bears here. And if we do, they'll probably be the cuddly kind."

With a half grin, he shook his head, then popped some berries into his mouth. "These are sweeter than I remember."

"Everything's sweeter here." She munched on a few, then gave him a deep kiss.

"*Nice.*" He'd become more like himself again. At ease.

"Thank you." She placed her hand against his chest. "I'm proud of you. You faced your fear, just like I did."

He turned and looked at his mare, which nosed around in the bushes munching on leaves. "I couldn't have done it without you."

"Do you think you'll have an easier time getting back on? I mean ... we didn't go very far."

"Sure." He seemed a little tentative at first, but then smiled broadly. "Yeah. I'm good."

"I'm here for you, Ryder." She gave him a quick peck. "So, when we go back and reach the field, let's let them run."

"I don't—"

"Nothing bad will happen." She moved to her horse, patted its nose, then mounted. "C'mon."

This time when he stepped into the stirrup, he definitely showed more confidence. He swung his leg up and over the horse like a pro. With reins in hand, he took the lead and led them out of the woods into the pasture.

The field opened up in front of them, and before she could blink an eye, Ryder let out a *whoop* and sped away at a full gallop.

She took her time following him, proud of what he'd accomplished. Her heart thumped, full of joy.

He's amazing.

"Yes!" he yelled. He leaned forward and pushed the horse even harder. "Freaking awesome!"

Amber bubbled with laughter and chased after him. The ground thundered under the horses' hooves and her heart beat steadily with it.

As Ryder slowed, she did, too. She couldn't take her eyes off him.

I love you.

He dismounted when he reached the stable, then sprinted to her side. "Thank you!" After helping her down, he swung her around in his arms and turned in two full circles. "I love you so much!" He covered her in kisses, and they fell down together onto a soft mound of grass.

"I love you more." She pushed him onto his back, ready to cuddle into his chest. A small white card lay in the grass close to his hip. "Ryder, I think this fell out of your pocket." She picked it up and handed it to him.

He held it in the air and shook his head. "Never be afraid to run." He gave it back to her. "My fortune. I think you should keep it. That gypsy might know more than what we gave her credit for."

"Yeah. You ran that mare pretty hard. You're not afraid of running at all anymore, are you Ryder?"

He glanced down at his legs. "Not one bit." He rolled her over. "Thanks to you."

She gazed up at him. "I want to stay here forever."

"On the ground?" He gave her that gorgeous half-grin.

"Funny." She ran a finger along his lips. "With you. I wanna stay with you."

"Then, stay." His grin went away, replaced with a much more serious expression.

If only it could be that simple.

CHAPTER 17

"Mom ..." Amber forced the word, but it barely came out. She gasped for air.

Unable to get louder, she struggled to pull the pillow out from behind her head. It might be the only way to get her mom's attention. She managed to pitch it sideways and knocked the lamp onto the floor.

It fell with a thump and luckily didn't break.

Better yet, it worked.

"Amber?" Her mom peered around the door, wide-eyed, then rushed to her side.

"I can't ... *Breathe*." She held her hand to her chest. All the times she'd thought she could be brave, but this terrified her.

"Try to calm down. Breathe in through your nose and out through your mouth." Her mom fidgeted with the oxygen tank that had been sitting in the corner of the room just waiting for this moment.

Amber had refused to use the thing, similar to the way she'd refused the walker. Each crutch took her one step closer to death and permanent separation from Ryder.

After mumbling a few choice words under her breath, her mom got the thing going. It gave off a low hum as well as the sound of bubbling water. She fumbled with the clear plastic tubes. "Okay. These go around your ears, and then this part goes in your nose." She positioned them into place. "Better?" Her brows drew together. She looked white as a sheet.

I'm not the only one scared to death.

Amber took a long breath through her nose. The pure oxygen calmed her and allowed her to breathe easily. "Yeah. Thanks, Mom."

Tears trickled down her mom's cheeks. Her chin vibrated out of control. With more pain in her eyes than Amber had seen yet, she turned around.

"It's okay," Amber whispered. "I can breathe now."

Her mom remained with her back to her. "Good."

"Mom. We knew this time would come."

"I'm not ready."

"You'll never be."

Finally, she faced her. "You're right." She sat beside her and took her hand. "Just stay with me as long as you can. Okay?"

Amber silently nodded. The oxygen had another effect. It made her sleepy. Her eyes drooped.

"You go on and sleep, baby." Her mom checked the oxygen tank, gave her a kiss on the forehead, and walked out. But she left the door wide open.

Amber closed her eyes.

* * *

A cold nose nudged Amber's cheek.

"Hello, girl." She stroked the mare's side, then reached into her pocket. *Empty.* "Sorry, no apples today."

Where's Ryder?

Sunlight streamed a sparkling ray through an opening in the trees. She found herself in the middle of some pretty dense woods. Trees surrounded her. Her mom had fussed at her over a lesson in dendrology. Amber had told her she couldn't care less what the different types of trees were. To her they were all pine trees.

She bent down and picked up a pinecone.

Yep, pine trees.

Dressed in jeans and a t-shirt, she was comfortable. It was plenty warm, but a feeling of panic struck her. She'd never felt so alone in her dreams. The horse eased her a little, but it didn't help when it pawed nervously at the ground.

"Me, too." She ran her hand along the mare's nose. "Let's get going."

Instead of mounting, she took the reins and led the animal along a dirt path through the woods. Bees buzzed in and out of thick orange honeysuckles, and birds chirped in the branches above her.

Like the pasture, this place was unfamiliar. It wasn't unpleasant, but being without Ryder left her empty.

She startled and jerked when a doe ran across the path in front of her. About twenty feet away, it stopped and looked at her. Its huge eyes stared without blinking, but also without fear. Then, it darted away.

"Beautiful," she muttered.

"Yes, you are." Ryder's arms encircled her from behind. He pushed aside her hair and kissed her neck, then turned her to face him.

"Ryder!" She squeezed him hard, then pulled his head down and gave him a good long kiss.

"Well hello to you, too." He swayed with her in his arms.

No way would she risk him disappearing, so she linked her fingers into the belt loops at the back of his jeans and yanked him against her. "I'm just glad I found you. I didn't like being out here alone."

Her action prompted an enormous grin. "You found me? No, I found you."

"That again?" She matched his grin. "This feels like *deja vu*. Let's just say we found each other."

"Ah. The girl speaks French."

"*Oui*." She laughed out loud and kissed him again.

The forest didn't seem the least bit scary anymore. It was even a little brighter.

Her mare had gone ahead on her own, following Ryder's horse. She wasn't worried. Now that Ryder had come, she felt totally safe.

"So, where were you?" she asked, looking up into his eyes.

"Getting things ready."

"Things? What things?"

"Patience, my dear girl. If you'll release me, I'll show you."

She knew his playful tone well.

What's he up to?

She reluctantly let him loose, and he took her hand.

"Come with me," he said.

They walked along the path, which followed a small stream. The pleasant sound of running water made her thirsty. "You don't happen to have something to drink, do you?"

"Only the freshest water around. C'mon."

He took her off the path to the stream, then knelt down and scooped water into his hand and took a long drink. "Ah ... Perfect."

"Is it safe? I mean, will I get sick if I drink it?"

He shook his head. "I wouldn't have drunk it if it wasn't. Remember. Nothing here is dangerous."

She knelt beside him and bent over the stream, then followed his example. She wasn't as good at it as him and slurped the water into her mouth. "Mmm. It's sweet."

"Knew you'd like it." He chuckled. "Here use this." He extended a metal cup.

"Nice." She dipped it into the cool water and filled it full, then drank every last drop.

"Feel better?"

"Definitely. I'm with you, aren't I?" She didn't have a care in the world.

They returned to the path and soon came to a large clearing. A humongous tree trunk surrounded by a fence stood at the center. Outside the fence, a blanket was spread on the ground.

"Where are we?"

"Ever heard of the Mullan tree?" He crossed to the fencing. "That's it." He pointed over his shoulder.

She went and stood beside him. "I heard they got rid of it. That only a plaque remained where it once was."

"You know your history."

"I know a lot about Coeur d'Alene. Kids used to joke about it. I heard guys liked to bring girls up here parking by luring them to see the stupid thing. Then, when they got here and there wasn't anything special, it was a good excuse to just make out."

Ryder's shoulders slumped, and he pointed to the blanket. "You just spoiled my plan."

She narrowed her eyes and gave him her most vicious look. "You're not turning rotten on me, are you?"

"Never. I just love to tease you."

She butted up against him. "You can still kiss me if you want."

"I plan to. But first things first. We need to eat."

"Eat?"

He motioned again to the blanket. What had been an empty space now held a wicker picnic basket. "You like fried chicken, don't you?"

"Yeah. What else?"

"Let's look." He took a seat beside the basket and lifted the lid. Then he started hauling out the contents. "Hmm ... Potato salad—something every Idaho picnic has to have." He winked. "Grapes. Baked beans. And you're going to love this ..."

"What?"

He pulled out a large Tupperware container. "Chocolate cake."

"Yes!" She plopped down beside him. "Dessert first?"

"No." He shook his finger, strangely like her mom. "Save that for last."

He handed her a plate, and she filled it full. Whoever cooked the food did an awesome job. Everything had been seasoned to perfection. After they ate plenty, she pointed to the cake and fluttered her lashes.

"You're something else," he said, laughing.

He dug into the basket and brought out two small paper plates, then sliced into the cake. Her mouth watered, anticipating the chocolate indulgence. Not only was the *cake* chocolate, but the frosting was also thick *dark* chocolate.

He placed a slice onto a plate and waved it in front of her face. "You sure you want this? It might not be good." His finger dipped into the frosting, then he licked it clean and smacked his lips. "Not *too* bad."

"Let me try."

He got another glob of frosting on his finger, and she opened her mouth. Thinking back to his trick with the cotton candy, she decided to be just as bold. She closed her mouth around his finger, then slowly pulled back. "Mmm ... You lied. It's delicious." She swirled her tongue around her lips.

He gaped at her.

"What?" She gave him her best attempt yet at being totally coy.

"Come here." He bade her forward with his damp finger.

They kissed. The most delicious chocolate kiss ever.

Amber devoured her cake. She'd never had something so rich and wonderful.

"What do you suppose that's for?" She pointed to a yellow ribbon tied around a distant tree.

He cocked his head and stood. "My dad and I used to put ribbons like that around trees when we'd go hiking, so we wouldn't get lost."

She pushed off from the ground and walked toward it. "Maybe we're not alone."

"We're *usually* alone." He fingered the ribbon, then tipped his head and nodded farther up the path. "I see another one." He pointed. "It's quite a ways away. Do you see it?"

She squinted. "Yeah, I do. Why don't we follow them?"

"Could be fun." He took her hand. "What if we find someone at the other end?"

"They can't hurt us, right?"

"Right."

She glanced over her shoulder. "What about the leftover food? It might draw in some bears."

"What food?" He nodded to where they'd been. Everything had vanished. Even the blanket and basket.

"No problem then." She shrugged, and they headed down the path.

The walkway twisted and turned and climbed gradually upward. But they managed it with ease and were thoroughly enjoying themselves. They talked and laughed, and every time they thought they'd come to the end of the line, another yellow ribbon appeared on a distant branch.

"Coeur d'Alene forest is huge," Amber said. "But I think we're gonna walk the whole thing if we keep this up."

"You tired?"

"No. Not at all." She squeezed his hand. "This is fun."

The trail got steeper. Ryder took the lead. "I think we're almost at the top."

"Good. Do you see more ribbons?"

"One. About fifty more feet."

She hooked her fingers in his belt loops and let him pull her along.

The trail led them to an old logging road. They saw no sign any trees had been removed, but there were deep ruts in the road, as if a truck had recently come by.

"Look at those trees," Amber said. Two pine trees criss-crossed and formed an X.

"Cool."

They walked over to the unusual growth, and Ryder ran his hand along the bark. "Someone carved their initials here inside a heart."

"Romantic. Maybe we should carve ours, too." When he moved his hand, she grunted. "That's too weird." She stepped a little closer to the tree. Her foot rolled over a rock, and she stumbled.

He quickly grabbed her arm and kept her from falling. "What's weird about it?"

"Those initials. C.S. and C.T. were my parent's initials. Clark Stewart and Carol Tyler."

"Not so weird. I'm sure there are lots of people with those initials."

"Yeah, but ..." The butterflies in Amber's belly told her something else. She traced the deep cuts in the wood with her finger. "I think we were supposed to find this. The yellow ribbons stopped right here."

Ryder winced, then put his hand over his eyes. "Did you see that?"

"What?"

His eyes pinched tight. "There's something really bright down there." He pointed over the side of the mountain into the brush.

She looked to where he'd pointed, and then she, too, saw a gleam of light. "The sun's reflecting off something." She moved closer to the edge.

"Be careful. I don't want you to fall."

"You said we're safe here."

"We are. But that doesn't mean you should purposefully do something dangerous." He held onto her with a death grip.

"Don't you want to know what it is?"

"Sure. But I don't want you to break your neck finding out."

Curiosity had gotten the best of her, but he made sense. And even though she was sure a broken neck wasn't possible, she definitely didn't want to ruin their perfect day. This side of the mountain was thick with brush and dense trees and too steep to climb down. She couldn't figure out a way to get to the shiny object.

"Okay," she said. "Hold onto my hand while I lean out and try to get a better look."

He wrapped an arm around one of the trees, then held onto her arm with his other hand.

She leaned way out. "Wow."

"What?"

"There's something buried under the trees. I think it's been there a while."

"Can you tell what it is?"

She shifted a little to the left and gasped. "It's a car. The light you saw was reflecting off the chrome bumper." She looked over her shoulder. "You think someone went off the road?"

"If there's a car down there, that would be a pretty obvious conclusion."

"Smarty." She wanted to call him much worse, but it didn't seem appropriate here. "What if someone's still in there?"

"Amber. The car's buried under years of growth. No way someone's still inside. And if they are, they're not breathing."

This time she moved to the right. "Yep. I can see part of a license plate. I see a K and the numbers one and seven. From what I can see of the car it's bright red. But most of it's buried."

He hauled her up.

"It's just awful." She shook her head. "I mean. What a horrible way to die."

"How do you know someone died? They might have gotten out. This happened a long time ago."

Time here was so unpredictable she wasn't certain when it might have happened. "I think we were supposed to find it. You know. The yellow ribbons and all."

"But why?" He craned his neck and peered over the ledge.

"I don't know." Her eyes shifted to the ground at her feet. "What's this?" She bent down and picked up a small white rectangular card.

Ryder stood over her shoulder. "Isn't that the fortune you got at Playland Pier?"

"Yeah. So weird." She scanned the card.

You'll find what you lost.

"Amber!"

Her mom hovered above her.

"No!" Amber gasped for air.

CHAPTER 18

"Mom, why'd you wake me up?" Amber inhaled the pure oxygen and tried to calm down.

"You were tossing around in bed, and the oxygen tube came out of your nose. And ... You were saying that boy's name." Her mom yanked at the blankets. "I don't like it. Not one bit."

Amber was in no mood to argue with her. Whether she liked it or not, there wasn't anything she could do about it. Her time with Ryder was hers alone. No one could interfere. With every dream she fell deeper in love with him.

This last one had been different than the others. Sure, they still enjoyed kisses and no matter what they did, she wanted it to last forever. But this dream had been more serious than the others. Why had they been led to that car? And why did her fortune card show up there? She'd not found anything she'd lost.

Amber looked up into her mom's eyes. "What?" She'd been glaring at her.

"You've been staring right through me. Don't you have something to say for yourself?"

"Really?"

"I told you I don't like the dreams you're having. They're obviously upsetting you. If I hadn't come in, you could've died." Her mom grabbed a tissue and blew her nose.

"So what do I do? Stop dreaming?" Amber slapped her in the face with a bit of sarcasm. After all, she'd asked for it.

What a stupid thing for her to be mad about. How am I supposed to stop my dreams?

"I'm calling Dr. Carmichael." Her mom stood up straight and jerked her nose into the air—her way to cope with Amber's attitude. "I'll get him to change your meds. Or at least give you something to help you sleep through the night."

"Fine. Go for it."

Sleeping through the night was exactly what she wanted to do.

Bring on the sleeping pills.

With a huff, her mom walked out.

Maybe she shouldn't have gotten so snarky, but she'd acted ridiculous. Of course, Amber immediately hated herself for being rude to her. It'd always been their pattern.

They'd get along fine for a while, but then something would have them at each other's throats again.

Having her criticize the only good thing about her life right now had set Amber on edge. Still, this wasn't how she wanted to end her time with the person who'd brought her into the world. The only one on earth who'd given her life. Aside from her dad. But his job had been a lot easier.

He'd probably enjoyed putting her there, but her mom had to go through the pain of childbirth. Then he left them before things got really tough, and her mom had to go it alone. Whether Amber liked it or not, she owed her everything. No doubt she loved her mom, and her mom loved her. Maybe that's why they argued. They were both pissed that all of this happened.

Parents aren't supposed to watch their kids die. Kids are supposed to grow up and give them grandchildren.

Everything had been turned upside-down. Totally wrong.

She'd be sure to apologize, but not until after she'd taken a good nap.

* * *

"Hey! Watch this one!" Ryder yelled.

Amber took in her surroundings and happily discovered they were once again at his dad's ranch. She breathed deeply. The sweet earthy scent of grass and horses covered her.

"You watching?" he hollered again.

"Are you crazy?" She covered her mouth with her hand and burst out laughing.

The guy stood on his hands on top of his horse, riding at a slow gallop. He'd definitely gotten over his fear. He looked like a real cowboy with chaps and a leather vest.

Hot and sexy.

"Woo-hoo!" He flipped in the saddle and landed on his butt, then pushed the horse into a full run.

After admiring her own cowboy boots, Amber perched on the fence rail and watched him ride around the perimeter.

Greatest show on earth. Forget Barnum and Bailey.

"Ride it, little cowboy!" She removed the hat from her head and waved it in the air.

"How about this one?" In a swift move, Ryder rotated in the saddle and rode backward. The horse continued at a full gallop.

"Ryder! Remember what you told me about doing something dangerous?" She yelled out after him, but he kept on going.

He can't get hurt here ... He can't get hurt here ...

She repeated it over and over in her mind.

Finally, he righted himself in the saddle and rode toward her. He jumped down, then patted his horse on the rump and sent her on her way. As she ran, her saddle vanished. Here, taking care of horses was almost too simple.

Amber climbed over the fence and into the pasture. "You know you're a little insane, don't you?"

He lifted her off the ground. "It's your fault." He laughed, kissed her, and set her down.

"My fault?"

"Yep. You got me back in the saddle. I'd watched my dad for years do all those tricks and I never could. But now ..."

"You're making up for it." She licked her lips and moved in close. "You're pretty incredible."

"So are you. We're in this together."

She studied his face. "What are we into?"

He lowered his head, but then raised it again. A warm smile accentuated his dimple. "I think we met so we could help each other. I helped you get over your fear of water and heights, and you helped me ride." He wound his finger around a strand of her hair. "Sometimes we have to be pushed to do things we don't want to do."

His simple touch turned into much more. All of his fingers raked through her hair and glided along the length. She closed her eyes. "That feels so good."

His lips touched hers with a sweet kiss.

When she opened her lids again, she found his face still close to hers. Tears glistened in his eyes.

"Ryder?" She touched his cheek. "What's wrong?"

"Nothing. Absolutely nothing."

"Then why ..." She wiped a tear away that had fallen onto his face.

"I never thought I could be so happy. My life hasn't been easy. Yet with you ..." He kissed her forehead. "Don't ever leave me."

She held onto him with every ounce of strength in her body. "I won't."

"You won't what?"

Her mom's face had replaced Ryder's.

"Mom?" The thrum of the oxygen tank brought her back to reality.

Reality sucks.

"You were talking in your sleep again. Yelling out that boy's name. This has gotten out of hand."

Before trying to talk, Amber took a deep breath. "The dreams are good. They aren't hurting me."

Her mom shook her head. "Not hurting you?" She pointed a rigid finger at the oxygen machine. "That's keeping you alive right now. Maybe you're purposefully taking the tubes out of your nose. I don't know! But every time I come in here, I have to put them back in. You look awful. You claim to sleep, but the bags under your eyes tell me otherwise."

"What does it matter?" Amber didn't have the strength to argue.

"It matters because you're my daughter and my responsibility. I told Dr. Carmichael I'm capable of caring for you. He wanted me to take you to the hospice house, but I don't want your final days to be in a strange place surrounded by people who don't know you. They don't love you like I do!"

"Mom." *Please don't yell at me.* "I don't wanna go there."

"Good. At least we can agree on something." She let out a long sigh, then wiped across her brow with the back of her hand.

Once her mom calmed down, Amber thought about everything she'd said. The words *final days* hit hard.

Is it really that close?

She breathed deeply through the tubes. Her mom had also mentioned discussing hospice care again.

Am I ready?

"Since you're awake," her mom said, completely recomposed. "I'd like to change your bedding. Think you can sit in the chair?"

"Yeah."

Her mom scooted it closer to the bed so the tubes from the oxygen tank would still reach. She pulled back Amber's blankets then helped her into it. Kneeling on the floor, she tucked a blanket around her legs and feet. Her hands lingered for a moment on one of Amber's heels.

"Your feet are so cold," she mumbled and pushed the quilt around Amber's legs. Then she dug into the dresser drawer, yanked out a pair of thick socks, and put them on Amber's feet.

After she stripped the bed, she tossed the bedding onto the floor. She then began to remake it with clean sheets. Amber had seen this process many times, but her mom moved slower than usual. Maybe she felt as exhausted as her. Since she'd been coming into her room every time she dreamed now, her mom hadn't been sleeping. Or if she had, it wasn't deep sleep, or she wouldn't so easily be waking up.

The doorbell rang.

Her mom popped rigidly upright. "I'll get it."

Dumb thing to say.

With a leap over the mound of dirty bedding, her mom sped away.

Amber strained to hear what was happening in the other room.

Her mom returned, smiling. "That was the delivery service. Dr. Carmichael has prescribed some new meds. Something to help you sleep."

Yes!

She ripped the bag open and yanked out the bottle. After examining the label, she opened the lid and dispensed the meds into her hand. "I'll get you some bread so you won't be taking this on an empty stomach."

She walked out, then came back before Amber could blink twice. She handed her a slice of bread, then placed two pills on Amber's tongue and gave her a glass of water.

"Amber, I hope this helps. You need your sleep."

So do you.

"Thanks, Mom."

Amber managed to eat all the bread and prayed the meds would work fast. The sooner she returned to Ryder, the happier she'd be.

Her mom quickly finished remaking the bed. Somehow she'd gotten a burst of energy. Then she helped Amber get under the covers. After securing the oxygen tubes, she patted Amber's cheek and left the room.

Amber nestled deeper into the pillows. She shut her eyes and inhaled the pure air.

Ryder, I'll be with you soon.

CHAPTER 19

"Good morning."

"Huh?" Amber's eyes popped open.

"I said, good morning. Did you sleep well?" Her mom's fingers brushed across her cheek as she ran them along the oxygen tubes. "Perfect. Stayed right where they belong."

Amber blinked hard several times until her mom came into focus. Her vision was blurrier than normal. "I ... uh." She rubbed her hand over her head, confused. "I slept?"

"Yes. All night. I didn't hear a sound from you. When I came in this morning you hadn't moved. Must have slept pretty heavy." She grinned.

There's no way I slept all night.

She tried to push herself up in bed, but struggled.

"I'll help." Her mom slipped an arm behind Amber's back and hoisted her up. "Need to pee?"

"Yeah." Any day now she expected to see a stranger in the house. A hospice nurse who'd put in a catheter and have to change her like a baby.

Not yet.

With her mom's help, she trudged at a snail's pace to the bathroom, then back into bed again. Her mom put the oxygen tubes back in place, patted the blankets around her, then tucked in the edges. "What's wrong, baby? You seem out of sorts."

"I don't understand."

"What?"

"I can't remember dreaming."

"Oh." She smiled. "That's probably a good thing. Like I said, you slept soundly."

"But ..."

No.

If she mentioned Ryder, her mom would go ballistic. "I like to dream."

She didn't comment. Instead, she patted her cheek, then kissed her on the forehead. "I'll fix you some breakfast then help you shower." She moved to the door. "I thought maybe I could watch a movie with you later. Would you be up for *Twilight* again?"

Wow. What changed her?

She acted a little like Mary Poppins. So cheerful she was almost scary.

"Sure." Amber was always ready to watch *Twilight*. Of course, if they got started on the first one, they'd have to watch all of them. She'd take advantage of her mom's changed disposition.

With a huge smile, she left the room, but not before patting the *Twilight* poster on the wall. Then, she started whistling.

Has she gotten into my meds?

Amber rolled her eyes, then studied the poster. Her mom knew it was one of her favorite movies—thus the outdated poster. Amber preferred the sequels and would've loved to have gotten one featuring Taylor Lautner. She'd never forget the way her heart fluttered when Jacob shed his shirt. *The same way I felt about Ryder.*

In many ways, Ryder and Jacob had a lot in common. Similar thick dark hair and incredibly muscular chests.

Bella totally screwed up when she picked Edward.

Her mom hadn't been gone five minutes and came back. "The movie might have to wait. Stephanie's going to stop by in a while. I called her and told her I thought it would be a good idea to come soon." This time, a sad smile, and she was gone again.

Major mood swings.

But then, reality struck again.

Mom knows I don't have much longer.

Amber pinched her eyes shut. Her mind had gotten so messed up she couldn't keep anything straight. She'd been distracted by her mom's weirdness, but now an even greater reality hit hard.

Why didn't I dream?

For months she'd shared every night with Ryder. One night apart, and she wanted to cry.

She gasped for air in a sudden panic. Trying to calm herself, she breathed deeply. Unstoppable tears filled her eyes.

I'm as crazy as Mom.

She tried to piece things together. Christmas had come and gone—as well as the New Year. But she couldn't re-member anything special about them. The only thing that mattered anymore was her time with Ryder.

She thought hard. He'd been doing tricks on his horse. She could visualize him perfectly. Upside-down on top of the black mare. Laughing. So happy ...

And many, many kisses.

Please let me sleep.

Refreshed from the pure oxygen, she dozed off.

"Amber." Her mom gently shook her shoulders. "Stephanie's here."

"What?"

"Stephanie's here."

Amber blinked, scrunched her eyes tight, then blinked again. Her heavy eyes didn't want to open. "What about?" Big breath. "Breakfast?"

"You were sleeping so deeply when I came in with it, I took it back to the kitchen."

Good. I don't wanna eat anyway.

"How long ... did I sleep?"

"Five hours." She helped Amber into an upright position. "But it's good. Your body needs rest." Huge smile and a pat on the cheek. "All right. I'll be right back with Stephanie." She left the room.

Five hours?

Still no dreams. No Ryder. Panicked, she breathed hard and fast.

Why?

Her mom returned holding a glass of water and two slices of bread. "Eat the bread, then I'll give you your pills. Once you've taken them, I'll send Stephanie in." She handed Amber the bread.

Amber ate as fast as she could, but her nerves were shot. Though eating didn't appeal to her, at least she'd have something on her stomach to keep the medicine from being thrown up again. Maybe once Stephanie left, she could sleep again. She *had* to see Ryder.

Her mom just stood there, grinning. Once Amber had choked down the bread, she handed her two pills. Amber dutifully took them and polished off the entire glass of water. Of course, her hands shook so bad, her mom had to hold it to her lips. But the cool water helped.

"Good girl." She flashed another smile and walked out.

"Amber?" Stephanie came in. Her eyes widened, then she quickly turned her head. She covered her mouth and burst out crying.

"Steph?"

The girl turned completely around so her back was to Amber. She sniffled and sobbed.

If the jerk hurt her ...

"Steph." Amber could only get a few words out at a time, but she'd keep on until Stephanie told her everything.

"Oh, Amber!" Stephanie rushed to her side. She draped herself over Amber's body, crying harder than ever.

I'll rip the hair out of his head.

Amber tried to remain calm. Getting upset would make breathing even harder. "What happened?"

Stephanie raised her head. "Huh?"

"What happened ... to you?"

She licked her lips and stared. "To *me*? Nothing happened to me. I'm crying because ..." She sucked in air and sniffled again. "You look terrible."

"Thanks." Amber did her best to smile.

"I'm sorry. But all those ..." She swirled her hand through the air and pointed to the tubes. "Those *things*. It's horrible."

"It helps."

Stephanie yanked a tissue from the box on the dresser and blew her nose. Acting like she might need oxygen herself, she took a few large breaths, then grabbed the chair, scooted it closer to the bed, and sat. "I'm glad it helps you." She twisted her fingers together. "Does it hurt?"

"Pain meds." Another forced smile.

"Good. I don't want you to hurt."

"How 'bout you?" Amber inhaled as much oxygen as she could, preparing to get upset.

"Me?"

"Jason." She hated saying his name.

"Oh." Her mouth twitched, then she dropped her head and stared at her hands. "He's fine."

A major change from Thanksgiving when she'd said *I think I'm in love* and had wriggled on her bed. This wouldn't be good. She knew Stephanie well enough to read her body language like a book. "Tell me."

She rolled her eyes. "I think he wants to be with Susan Adams."

"Susan?" The girl with the worst reputation at the high school.

"Yeah. She was hanging all over him at the basketball game Friday night."

"And ..."

Stephanie shrugged. "I thought he loved *me*."

No, Jason loves Jason. He used you, Steph.

Amber slowly reached out to her. "Sorry."

Stephanie took her hand and gave it a squeeze. She'd recovered from bawling, but tears still dripped down her face. "What guy'll want me now?"

"What?"

Such a dumb thing to say. You're beautiful, smart, and more fun than that ass Jason.

Stephanie looked toward the window. "I'm not a virgin anymore."

"Oh."

"I can't believe I did it with him."

I can.

"It's okay," Amber rasped.

Stephanie tightened the hold on her hand. "No, it's not. I mean, I'm on the pill. So I didn't get pregnant or anything. But I'm sure he told his friends. They look at me different." Tears fell down her cheeks. "Austin Peterson smacked his lips when I walked by him going to my locker. They all must think I'm easy now." She let go of Amber's hand, then pulled more tissues from the box and wiped her eyes.

There'd been a time when Amber thought she wanted to know what it was like. To have Stephanie share all the sordid details. But now, she didn't want to know any of it. What she'd done with Jason hurt her. Hopefully it wouldn't make her as bitter and scarred as her mom had been all these years. Listening to Stephanie was like listening to her mom all over again. "It's not right."

"Guess not. But I could've told him *no*. I just really thought he loved me. He told me it'd make our feelings stronger. Talked about how one day he'd marry me. Yeah, right. Now I think he wants to see just how *strong* he can make it with Susan. Doubtful he'll propose marriage to her."

"He's an ass."

Stephanie covered her mouth, then started to laugh. But within seconds, she started to cry again. "What am I gonna do without you?" She grabbed Amber's hand and squeezed it like a vice.

"*Live*." Amber could barely keep her eyes open.

"Oh, sweetie. You look so tired."

"I *am*."

Stephanie stood. "I should go."

"No. Not yet."

I'm never gonna see you again.

"K." She sat back down with a sigh. "Cool picture." She held up the photo of Playland Pier. "I heard this place was awesome."

"It was." Amber closed her eyes, recalling the memory. More awesome than Stephanie would ever know.

She drifted ... A kiss on her cheek reopened her eyes.

"I'm gonna go. You need to sleep." Stephanie pinched her lips tight—no doubt choking back more tears. This time the jerk had nothing to do with it.

I make everyone cry.

"Amber, I love you. I'll never, ever forget you."

"I love you, too." Amber reached out to her. "It's okay." Big breath. "I'm not afraid."

"*I* am."

"Steph?" Amber deeply inhaled.

"Yeah?"

"Real love exists." Another deep breath. "Look for it."

Stephanie hugged her, then ran from the room in tears.

Amber shut her eyes and listened to the muffled sound of her mom and Stephanie talking.

Good. Maybe they can help each other through this.

So, so tired ...

CHAPTER 20

No...

Tears trickled from the corners of Amber's eyes as her mom opened the blinds. Another dreamless night.

"Honey? Why are you crying?" She grabbed a tissue and dabbed at Amber's eyes.

Amber stared blankly forward and took large breaths through the tubes in her nose.

Her mom pressed a firm hand to Amber's forehead. Her eyes widened, and she fled the room.

Within seconds, her voice filtered in through the walls. "Yes. This is Carol Stewart." She had a horrible habit of talking overly loud on the phone. For once, a good thing. Still, Amber had to strain to hear her over the noise from the oxygen machine.

"I think it's time ... No, not warm. Extremely cold."

Amber's heart thumped.

"Yes. I understand."

I'm scared.

"Uh-huh. Fine. I'll be waiting."

Her mom's bedroom door slammed shut. Even through the closed door her wailing shook the house.

Every ounce of bravery she'd had drifted away with her mom's tears.

I don't wanna die without seeing Ryder again.

Too weak to do anything else, she slept.

* * *

Whose hand?

Amber forced her lids open. A thin, cold hand removed the plastic tubing.

"I see you're awake." A strange smile on an even stranger face.

Amber blinked, but said nothing.

"Are you comfortable?"

Amber looked away from the woman. She looked older than her mom and a lot bigger, but they probably bought their scrubs at the same store. Light pink with white daisies.

"I'm Pam. I'm a nurse, and I'm here to help you. I'm changing your oxygen."

She'd seen the nametag. Pam, the hospice nurse.

So, it had come down to it. Her final weeks. She always thought she wouldn't know. She didn't *want* to know.

I need my mom.

"I gotta pee." She managed to say what seemed to be the most important thing.

The nurse's brows drew in with a horribly pitiful expression, and she patted Amber's arm. "Go on then. Don't you remember? I put in a catheter."

No.

Amber scrunched her face together and closed her eyes.

Is my body so messed up I can't even feel the stupid thing?

Pam patted her again. "It's okay, hon. It'll make it easier for you."

Amber couldn't stop her chin from quivering or the tears from coming down in a steady stream.

"Want me to bring your mom in?"

She nodded.

The moment she saw her, Amber stretched out her hand. "Mom ..."

She sat on the edge of her bed and held Amber's hand. "I'm here, baby."

"A catheter?"

"It was necessary. You'll get used to it."

For once she wanted her mom close. Someone she could hold onto. Someone she knew. "I didn't want it."

"I know." She looked like she'd cry any second now. She kept a tight hold on Amber's hand and with her free hand stroked Amber's head. "But we have to trust her. Dr. Carmichael said she's one of the best."

"Okay." Amber's lids got heavier. It was impossible to keep her eyes open. "I'm tired, Mom."

"You sleep, baby. The nurse will be back in a minute with more oxygen. I'll be close by."

You're always close by.

Maybe she should've appreciated her more these past years. Not taken her for granted.

I could've acted better.

Amber drifted, but not in sleep. Her new medicine made her dizzy. She felt like the bed spun in circles.

"Mrs. Stewart, you know our rules."

The nurse was in the other room with her mom. With the oxygen tank turned off, Amber heard her loud and clear.

"Yes, I know." Her mom sounded totally irritated. "You prescribe all meds."

"That's right. And this particular medication isn't on our list."

"I don't care. She needs it. Dr. Carmichael prescribed it."

"It's *not* on the list." *Sounds like mom met someone just as stubborn.*

"You don't understand. It helps her sleep. She'd been having horrible nightmares and couldn't get a decent night's rest. The medicine keeps her from dreaming. I want her to have it. She *needs* it."

Horrible nightmares? Liar!

Amber's breathing turned to rapid panting.

She gave me something to stop my dreams?

She wanted to scream. More than anything she wanted to tell her mom exactly what she thought of her.

How could she do that to me?

"Mom!" She pushed out the word with all her remaining strength.

I trusted you.

The voices in the other room got even louder.

"Mrs. Stewart, we'll be giving her morphine. She'll have no trouble sleeping."

"Mom!"

Her face appeared in the doorway. "Amber?"

"Mom." Too angry to cry, Amber glared at her. "Why?"

"What?" She crossed the room and stood over her. With arms folded hard across her chest, she'd prepared for a fight. Probably still in battle mode from arguing with the nurse.

Though weak, Amber wouldn't be intimidated. "My dreams." Breathing was so difficult. She needed oxygen. "You. Stopped them."

"Oh, baby." She reached out to touch Amber's cheek, but Amber cringed and turned her head.

"No." Amber's chest tightened even more. "Why?"

Her mom drew back and refolded her arms. "You weren't being sensible. Believed in someone imaginary. You cried out for him and tossed in your sleep. It was interfering with your oxygen because the tubes wouldn't stay in your nose. I did it to help you."

"Help?" Amber leered at her, heaving with thick heavy breaths. "I hate you."

"Mrs. Stewart." Pam the nurse had perfect timing. "You'll have to move so I can hook up her oxygen."

Her mom backed away, then fled the room in tears.

Amber immediately wanted to call her back.

I shouldn't have said it.

Her mom had sacrificed years to take care of her. No matter how angry she felt or what she'd done to her, saying she hated her was wrong.

"Here you go." The nurse put the oxygen tubes back into place. "This'll help." Pam gave her a genuine smile. "Have your nightmares been that bad?"

"No." Amber grabbed her hand. "Don't make me take that medicine." Her words came out raspy, but she spit them out fast. Deep, deep breath. "Don't listen to her."

"You're in *my* care now. I'll give you the proper medication to make you as comfortable as possible."

"I want to dream."

The nurse didn't respond. She adjusted Amber's blankets and left.

Just like everyone else.

* * *

Complete darkness. The thrum of the oxygen tank steadily pulsed. Amber stared blankly into nothingness.

"Amber?"

"Yeah."

"I need to talk to you." Her mom turned on the lamp beside the bed.

Every breath now was an accomplishment. Amber's body grew weaker by the hour, but at least she felt no pain. Whatever the nurse had given her worked better than anything she'd taken before.

"I'm listening," Amber whispered.

Her mom remained silent. When Amber shifted her eyes to look at her, she beheld the ghost of a woman who'd always been so alive.

"Mom?" Inhale. "I'm sorry."

"No. Don't say it. I'm the one who's sorry. That's what I came in to tell you."

"Why did you ... do that ... to me?"

Amber startled when she took her hand, but she didn't pull away. "You have every right to hate me. I'm a mess, Amber. These past few months have—I don't know—played with my mind. Made me say and do things I'm ashamed of. I've lived for so long believing everything is black and white. Good and bad. Real and ... imaginary." She squeezed Amber's hand. "I wanted you to do the same."

She reached into the box of photos on the dresser, then sat on the bed as close as she could get to Amber. "I know you didn't see all of these. I wanted to be sure you saw the ones I took of you and your dad."

A glimmer of light lifted Amber's spirit. For once her mom didn't sound bitter talking about him.

She held a photo in front of Amber's face. "Look here. I took this when you'd just taken your first steps."

Her dad was kneeling beside her, and she stood fully up-right clutching onto his extended fingers. It was hard to tell who had the bigger grin.

"He was so proud of you, Amber." Her mom smiled. The real kind of smile Amber remembered from long ago. "You walked at ten months. A little earlier than most ba-bies. I guess you just wanted to get your life going."

Maybe I knew it would be short.

One by one she showed her every picture and described each in detail. In every shot, both she and her dad had huge smiles. Some of the photos were staged, but most were candids.

"He loved you so much." Her mom started to cry again.

One day there will be no more tears.

"I hope you can forgive me for blaming you," her mom whispered.

"Huh?"

"I could've been a better mom. But deep down inside I blamed *you* because he left. And you were just a little girl ..." Sobs erupted from her. "It wasn't your fault." She lay down across Amber's body and shook with every sob. "I've been so bitter. Only because a day didn't go by that I didn't think of him."

She rose up, sniffling and breathing hard. "You asked me what it was like to fall in love. I had it with him. When you were born you meant *everything* to both of us.

"When he left ..." She struggled to continue. Her face contorted with every word. "A part of me died." She turned away.

"Mom." Her heart ached for her. "It's okay. I understand."

"No, it's not okay. I was unfair to you. I didn't think he'd leave for good. I thought he loved me. Just needed to cool off, and then he'd come home." She blew out a couple of long breaths and wiped her nose. Then she dug into the photos again. "Look at you here. Your dad was so protective of his car. Always afraid it would get scratched. But he let you stand on the back of it for this photo."

Amber gasped. Her hands shook out of control as she reached for it.

No way ...

"Baby? What's wrong?" Frantically, her mom examined the tubing. "Are you getting enough air?"

"That car." Her breathing grew even more rapid. The photo clearly showed the license plate on the bumper of a bright red car. K 20157.

"What about it?"

Amber had to calm down or she'd hyperventilate. "I saw it."

Her mom's face puckered, and she gaped at her like she'd gone completely nuts. "You couldn't have. You were too little to remember it."

"I saw it." *Breathe.* "In the woods."

"You're not making sense. I'm calling the doctor." She started to rise.

"No!" Somehow she managed to yell the word.

Her mom stopped. "What's gotten into you?"

"Dad's car ... In the woods ... Close to Mullan tree."

Her mom's demeanor totally changed. Her shoulders dropped, and her brow dipped low. "The Mullan tree?"

"Uh-huh."

"Did I ever tell you he proposed to me there?"

"No."

She nodded. "He drove me there." A far-off look in her mom's eyes gave Amber hope.

Maybe she'll believe me.

"What happened?"

"It was one of our best dates." She smiled, but kept her eyes focused downward. "I'd had bad memories of being driven into the woods by a boy. I told you about that. So when he went there, I was nervous at first. But then, he took a picnic basket from the trunk and spread a blanket on the ground."

Amber's heart thumped hard.

"We had fried chicken and potato salad. And then for dessert—"

"Chocolate cake?"

Finally, her mom looked at her. "How did you know?"

"Good guess."

Another smile. "Well ... stuck in the top of the cake— covered in frosting—was a ring. He asked me to marry him. Of course I said yes, and then he slid it on my finger." She laughed softly. "He took my finger in his mouth and licked off the frosting. It made my heart beat so hard."

Her mom's eyes closed, and tears fell silently down her cheeks. They were different from all the sobbing she'd just done. Her demeanor had softened from the happy memory she'd shared.

You're remembering how much you loved him.

"After he proposed we hiked up the hill to an old logging road. There were these trees there. Crossed over each other like an X."

"You put." Amber had to say it. She had to make her believe. "Your initials there."

"Yes. But how—"

"I saw it ... In my dream."

Staring, her mom stood and backed away. "How could you?"

"Don't know ... Dad's car ... Below those trees."

Her mom shook her head so fast it made Amber's spin. "No."

"Send someone. Please?"

"No. You're wrong. You can't dream real things. It's not possible."

Sometimes we have to be pushed to do things we don't want to do.

"Please?" Deep, deep breaths. "My *last* request."

Her mom defiantly crossed her arms. "But ..."

"I'm dying. Do this for me." Inhale. Exhale. "For *us*."

"Even if for some God-awful reason your dad wrecked his car and ..." She gasped. "*Died.* It wouldn't change a thing. He still walked out on us." Looking more confused than ever, she fled the room. Amber understood. No one asked for this emotional roller coaster ride.

But she's got to believe me.

Unable to keep her eyes open any longer, Amber drifted off to sleep.

CHAPTER 21

Amber curled her toes, then wiggled them in the warm sand. The familiar sound of seagulls brought her fully alert. Her heart pounded.

Is it possible?

"Amber!"

Ryder!

She spun around, and he almost knocked her to the ground.

He grabbed her and pulled her into his body, then kissed her all over her face with what felt like a hundred kisses. "I thought I'd never see you again." He finally kissed her lips, clutching her so tight he took her breath.

She cried, but not in pain. When she met his gaze, he, too, was crying. "I'm here," she whispered and kissed him. "I'm here, Ryder."

I'm back! Thank God, I'm back.

He grasped on to her, not letting go. They were alone on the city beach dressed in swimsuits and close to the water. Not far at all from where she'd almost died all those years ago. But she didn't care. It didn't matter where they were as long as they were together.

His skin felt so warm, his body firm and protective. She rested her head on his chest and breathed easily. Here she didn't struggle for every bit of air needed to keep her alive.

They dropped down onto a blanket spread on the sand.

He laid her back. "Where were you?" He licked his lips, and peered into her eyes. "I searched everywhere." The concern on his face wrenched her heart.

"I can't explain it. I wanted to be with you—tried to get here—but I couldn't."

"Don't leave me again. Without you here, everything was dark."

"But it's *never* dark here."

He stroked the side of her face, then ran his hand along her hair. "It was. Dark. Empty. Even cold. I'd never felt so alone. And then I saw you …" He sniffled. "I need you, Amber."

She put her hands behind his neck and brought him close, then kissed him with urgency. She didn't have much time left. "I want to stay with you, but I don't know how."

"Marry me."

"What?"

"I said, marry me. Be my wife. Stay with me forever."

"I want to. But—"

He put a finger across her lips. "Just say yes."

Could it be that easy?

Her answer was the biggest no-brainer of all time. "Yes."

She melted into the blanket as he rolled onto her and covered her with unending kisses.

"Ryder?" He had her breathless, but in a good way.

Did Mom feel like this when Dad proposed to her?

He moved to the side and propped himself up on one elbow, but made a point to keep his body touching hers. "Yes?" His warm hand rested on her belly.

"I don't think it was an accident that we met."

His fingertip traced the side of her face. "Of course it wasn't. You and I were always meant to be together."

"But ..." In no way did she want to discount what they had with each other. "It's more than that."

He drew back just a little. "You're being so serious. What's wrong?"

This is so hard.

She never wanted to bring anything bad with her here. No horrible memories. No pain. Definitely no mention of her illness. But she had to tell him this. It was too important not to.

"I didn't have the kind of dad you had."

"What?" He couldn't have looked more confused. Maybe he'd been expecting something much worse.

"My dad walked out on me and my mom when I was five. Just a few days after my accident. You know—when I almost drowned."

"Oh, baby. That's terrible. I'm so sorry." He smoothed her hair back from her forehead.

He'd called her *baby*. Just like her mom always had. But the way he said it made her tingle inside. Coming from *his* lips it felt fantastic.

She raked her fingers into his hair. "I'm sorry, too. Sorry I didn't know the truth. But I think I do now."

With a sparkle in his eyes and a nod of his head, he encouraged her to go on.

"That car we saw on the side of the mountain? I think it was my dad's."

"How do you know that?"

She gazed beyond him into the clear blue sky. So peaceful. It covered them in their perfect world. "My mom showed me a picture of me standing on the back of Dad's car. I could see the license plate. The numbers matched, and his car was red. Just like the one we found."

Ryder rubbed his chin like an old man would. "We were led there by the yellow ribbons." He looked up—obviously spinning it around in his mind—then became more affectionate again and stroked her cheek. "There's something incredible at work here, Amber. Greater than we realized. I doubt we're supposed to understand it. We're just supposed to accept it."

"I feel the same way. Still, it's important for me to know the truth." She peered into his eyes.

He bent down and kissed her. "You will."

"Amber." Her shoulders were being shaken.

When she opened her eyes, her mom bent in close. "Amber, baby. There's someone here to see you."

Amber's eyes were incredibly heavy. She wanted nothing more than to go back to sleep. Especially now. Now that she had no doubt Ryder was waiting for her.

She could hardly bring the person into focus. She blinked hard.

A man in uniform. He wore a long-sleeved olive-colored shirt with a dark green tie. But her eyes were drawn to his badge. She squinted.

Kootenai County Sheriff.

If she could, she'd jump from the bed and hug him. His being here led to only one possible explanation.

Mom believed me.

"Amber, this is Captain Murray. He knew your dad. They were friends." Her mom stepped to the back of the room, and the man moved closer.

"Hello, Amber." He had a nice voice. "I haven't seen you since you were a little girl. But I'm glad your mother called me."

"Hi." She struggled for every breath and every syllable.

He folded his hands in front of himself. The poor guy had to be uncomfortable. She wasn't exactly pleasant to look at. Then again, in his line of work, he'd probably seen worse.

"Your mother told me you had a dream about your father."

Now wait a minute. He'd started to sound condescending.

"His car," she rasped.

You'd better go find it, buddy.

Tears formed.

"Yes. Forgive me. I meant his car." His casually folded arms were now firmly crossed over his chest. "I can assure you, if there'd been an accident, we'd have discovered it long ago. The road you described is a well-traveled logging road. There's plenty of activity in that area. Someone would've seen it."

"No." Her heart raced. "It's there."

He shook his head. "It can't be."

"It *is.*"

He turned around and motioned for her mom to follow him out of the room.

No. Don't leave.

"Wait!" Tears rolled down her cheeks.

He stopped and faced her. His hardened features softened. "Amber, if I go out there and find nothing, won't that make it even worse for you?"

"I'm ... dying." Enormous breath. "Nothing ... will make ... it worse."

He put a hand over his mouth and lowered his head. "All right. I'll drive out there myself. Your mother told me about the trees. The ones with their initials." He looked over his shoulder at her mom. "I honestly don't expect to find anything. I've been out there myself before. But then again, that was back in high school. Before the two of you were married."

Probably went parking.

Her mom extended her hands to him. "Thank you, Carl. This means a lot to Amber."

His head bobbed up and down. "I'll let you know what I find."

"Captain Murray?" Amber pushed out his name.

"Yes?"

"Thank you."

With a warm smile, he walked out.

Relieved, Amber's heart slowed.

Her mom crossed to her and sat. "Honey, please don't get your hopes up too high. The whole thing is just ... *silly.* But since you wanted this, I called in a favor from an old friend."

"*Dad's* friend."

"He was my friend first. One of the few boys in school who treated me halfway decent." She fidgeted with her own fingers. "After those rumors spread about me, Carl stood up for me. He actually decked one of the football players who'd been teasing me in the cafeteria. Had him meet him in the parking lot one day after school. Put the guy on the ground."

"Cool."

"*Very* cool." She stroked Amber's face. "He's a good man."

"Thought you said ... no good men."

She shrugged.

Amber smiled.

Maybe there's hope for her.

"Baby, you go back to sleep now." She kissed her forehead. "Try to have sweet dreams."

"I will."

Amber closed her eyes.

CHAPTER 22

A thick fog surrounded Amber. So dense she could hardly see her hand when she held it in front of her face.

Where am I?

The distant hum of the oxygen machine was undeniable. But the tubes weren't in her nose. Still, she breathed easily.

I don't understand.

"Amber ..."

Ryder?

"Amber ..."

His voice echoed like something from her deepest dreams.

"Ryder? Where are you?" She yelled, but her voice came out barely more than a whisper.

She craned her neck and tried to see through the white cloud-like masses. Peering hard, she thought it might be him ahead of her, but a foggy mist cloaked everything.

Her feet weren't even touching the ground. She floated through the air.

It's like I'm walking on a cloud.

"Come back to me ..." Ryder's voice haunted her.

She clutched her chest.

God, it hurts.

Tears dripped from her eyes.

"I can't find you!" Her words came out as a garbled rasp. If only she could yell, he could come to her.

Something plastic slid between her lips, and a cool liquid covered the back of her tongue. A hand stroked her throat and made her swallow.

She forced her eyes open.

Nurse Pam leaned back. "Awake I see."

Amber couldn't utter a sound.

"I've given you something for the pain."

Amber shut her eyes again and drifted ...

* * *

"No!"

Amber's eyes popped wide. The shriek from the other room raced through her like a shot of adrenaline and sent blood pumping fast through her veins.

Her mom sobbed—*wailed.* She cried harder than she had on the day they'd gotten the worst news of their lives from Dr. Carmichael.

"Mom!" She couldn't push the word out hard enough.

I need you.

The nurse came in. After checking the oxygen machine, she ran a thermometer across Amber's forehead. Lastly, she took hold of her wrist and checked her pulse.

Pam smiled and inserted a plastic syringe into Amber's mouth. The liquid seeped out across her tongue.

"Can you swallow?" She followed her question by stroking Amber's throat. "Good girl."

"Mom." Amber tried to reach out, but she couldn't even lift her arm from the bed.

"I'll get her for you. She's had quite a shock, but I know she'll want to see you."

Amber expected to see her mom, but Captain Murray came in instead.

"Hello again, Amber." Not so condescending this time.

He nodded to the chair. "Mind if I sit?"

She blinked slowly.

With a smile—and no affirmative answer from her—he took it upon himself to sit.

He scratched his head. "I can't explain it."

Loud sobs continued from the other room.

"I went to the logging site." He swallowed hard, staring at the floor. "Not sure how no one ever saw it."

Dad's car.

She tried to still her heart, which had started to race as soon as the man sat. She inhaled deeply and attempted to ignore her mom's wailing, though it was nearly impossible. Amber's heart couldn't take much more.

He lifted his head. "You were right, Amber. It was your dad's car. Been on the side of that mountain for almost thirteen years now. We pulled it out. Towed it into town."

As weak as she was, her chin still quivered, and her tears fell. *They found it.* The thing the fortune teller had said she'd lost, and she hadn't known she'd lost it. That *thing* had been her dad. He'd always just been the man her mom despised—or *pretended* to. All this time he'd been lost, waiting to be found.

Even knowing this, it didn't explain how it happened. Truthfully, just like her mom had said, he'd walked out on them nonetheless. But how different would their lives have been if he hadn't left that day?

"I've heard about stuff like this. Folks dreaming things that happen. Psychics having visions that lead investigators to find missing people. But I've never dealt with anything that came anywhere remotely close to this before. It's all new to me." Again, he scratched his head. "All I know is, maybe you and your mom can rest a little easier now."

He froze and closed his mouth tight.

After glancing at the oxygen machine, he looked straight at her.

Are those tears in his eyes?

He sniffled, then wiped them with the heel of his hand. "Your mom has more to tell you. Once she calms down I'm sure she'll come in to see you."

"Amber." He stood. "Your dad was a good man. I'm sorry he didn't live to see you grown." He bent down and kissed her forehead, then jerked up and gave her an apologetic look. "Sorry. I have a daughter your age, and I just can't imagine ..." He wiped his eyes again.

Her mom was right. *He's a good man.*

Amber somehow managed to lift her hand. "Captain?"

He grasped onto it. "Yes?"

"I'm gonna be fine."

He squeezed a little tighter. "Yes, you are." With his other hand he patted their joined hands, then quickly left.

His loud bass voice mingled with her mom's.

Nurse Pam returned and once again took her temperature.

Amber struggled to breathe. Even with the oxygen.

The nurse walked out, but then came back in with her mom.

"There's not much longer," the nurse whispered. "If you have anything you want to say to her, Mrs. Stewart, you should do it now."

Not much longer ... Ryder ...

"All right." Her mom looked horrible. Her face glowed bright red, swollen from crying. She clutched a tissue in one hand and something else in the other.

"Tell me," Amber rasped.

Her mom burst into renewed tears.

The nurse leaned close to her. "Mrs. Stewart, you need to compose yourself. Tell her what she needs to hear." After giving her the firm advice, she left them alone.

Her mom sat as near to Amber as she could possibly get. "You were right. I don't know how you did it, but you knew."

I saw it, Mom.

"Carl—*Captain Murray*—thinks he probably swerved to miss a deer or something. Veered off the road and over the side of the cliff." She breathed deep, then sniffed. "At first I got mad. Assuming he was probably drunk. Regardless, I figured he was still leaving us. The fact he died wouldn't have forgiven his intent."

Her face contorted, and tears streamed. "But then, they found something in the glove compartment. They pulled out all the paperwork to confirm his registration. Make sure it was him. There was very little left of your dad." She placed her hand against her throat, nervously massaging it.

"They found this in there." She held up an envelope and removed a card, then drew a piece of paper from it. "This note was inside the card."

She sat up tall and took several large breaths. Then she smoothed the paper. "Let me read it to you."

She cleared her throat, then coughed. "My dearest Carol." Her voice shook with every word. "I'm such a fool.

I could have lost the most precious part of my life. And not only would *I* have lost her, but I would have taken her from you, too. How would you ever have forgiven me for the death of our daughter? I can't even forgive myself.

"I drove to Fourth of July Pass trying to get my head together. I'm writing this while staring at what used to be the Mullan tree. I'll never forget the day I asked you to marry me." She paused and blew her nose.

Amber needed a tissue, too. But she wasn't about to try and get her mom's attention to get her one. This was too important. She wanted to hear every word.

"You made me the happiest man in the world that day. There was only one day I know I was happier. The day you gave birth to our daughter. A living proof of our love, that will always exist. But because of me, that proof nearly died."

She stopped reading and shifted her gaze to Amber, then grabbed some tissues. She dabbed at Amber's eyes, then wiped it across her nose.

"Finish it," Amber whispered.

Her mom nodded, then found her place again in the letter. "Please forgive me. I'm done drinking. I'm going to try to be the most loving husband and the best dad I can be. I don't deserve either of you, but I want to come home. Tell me you'll forgive me, and let me love you forever. And if you can't, keep these to remember me. With all my love, Clark."

"What?" Her dad had written a beautiful letter.

He wanted forgiveness.

Her mom lifted the envelope from the dresser, then dumped the contents into her hand. Something shiny and silver dropped out.

She held up two matching silver heart-shaped lockets. "One for you and one for me." She burst out crying again, then pulled Amber into her arms.

"Oh, baby. He was coming home to us. He loved us." Her body jerked with heavy sobs.

If Amber had more strength, she'd be wailing right along with her, but she could only lie limply in her mom's arms. Too weak to hold on.

So little time left.

Amber had to tell her. "Find it again."

"What?"

"Love." Amber drifted, as if floating above the bed. "You don't ... have to ... be angry ... anymore."

"I wasted all those years hating your dad for something he didn't do. God, I'm so sorry!" She frantically smoothed her hands over Amber's head. "But loving again isn't possible."

"It is." Amber looked her in the eye. "Find it ... *I* found it." She blinked sluggishly; her heart beat slower. "You know ... it's possible."

"Yes." Her voice trembled with fear.

"I want ... to be with him."

"Him?"

"Ryder." Deep breath. "I love him." *So hard to speak.* She drew in a long breath. "He wants ... to marry me."

"That's good, baby." She stroked Amber's face, then grasped her hand.

"Don't ... be afraid. I ... know ... I'm going ... someplace better."

Her mom's face scrunched together. She clutched Amber's hand against her chest. "I love you, baby. Can you ever forgive me for ... *everything*? For being a lousy mom?"

"Nothing to ... forgive." With all her remaining strength, Amber squeezed her hand. "I love you, too."

"I love you so much." She kissed her hand, then leaned down and kissed her cheek. Quickly, she rose up, and her eyes darted here and there. "Do you remember when you were nine and we went to the circus?" Her words were spit out in a rush of frantic energy.

Amber was too weak to nod. "Yeah."

"I bought you a caramel apple and when you bit into it, the apple was rotten."

I remember.

"I tried to get the vendor to give us another one, but he said *no*. Said, *how was I supposed to know it was bad on the inside?*"

The memory came to her as vividly as if it had just happened.

"And you looked at me with your beautiful brown eyes and said, *it's okay, Mom. I'll just lick off the caramel. I like that part best anyway.*" She smiled, though tears lingered behind it. "You always looked on the bright side. Saw the best in things—in *people*, too. And when you got sick, you faced it with the same bright outlook. Believed you'd get better."

But I never did.

"When we tried to find a match for your bone marrow, I wanted to find your dad more than ever. I thought ... just *maybe* he could help. But I didn't know where to look."

It wouldn't have helped.

"And that was what was so hard to deal with. For the first time in your life, I watched your attitude change. That's when you became bitter, and it broke my heart because I couldn't fix it. I couldn't make you better—take away your pain. It's impossible to put a bandage on cancer." Her control was almost gone again. Her face scrunched tight. "Did I fail you?"

"No." Amber's eyes were half shut. "Let it go."

"I can't." She burst out with a loud sob. Her gentle hand stroked Amber's cheek over and over again.

"Yes ... you can." Amber floated. The sensation she'd grown accustomed to. "Let *me* go." She forced her eyes to open one last time.

Her mom's chin quivered, and she nodded.

"Ryder," Amber whispered.

"What, baby?"

Though Amber's arm felt like it was filled with lead, she managed to lift it from the bed and point with a half-bent arm. "He's there." He stood in front of her reaching out his hand. "Don't you ... see him?"

Her mom sobbed out of control, and clutched Amber's body tightly against her. She swayed back and forth. "I love you ... I love you ..."

Chapter 23

Familiar fingers entwined with Amber's. Radiant sunlight surrounded her. She closed her eyes and smiled, with her face lifted to the warmth.

"You aren't planning to back out on me now, are you?" Ryder raised her hand to his lips and kissed her knuckles.

"Back out on you?"

"Funny girl. You said yes. I made all the arrangements."

She took in everything around her. A little like the city park, but different. Lots of trees and grass. Soft music came from somewhere. The kind her mom used to listen to. Old love songs. "'Everything I Do.' I know this song."

"Like it?"

"Yeah, I do."

"Then walk with me." He grinned. His best one ever.

Right before her eyes, he changed from jeans and a t-shirt into a white tuxedo.

She looked down.

A wedding dress?

The type she'd always dreamed of wearing. Form-fitting white satin strung with tiny seed pearls. She touched her head. Baby's breath had been braided into her hair.

"You're beautiful, Amber." Ryder pulled her close for a kiss.

"Um … that's supposed to come *after* we say our vows." She bit her lower lip.

He tapped her mouth with a single finger. "Beautiful *and* cute. I'll give you another kiss after. And another. And another."

"So what are we waiting for?"

He extended his arm, and she linked hers through it.

They walked down a long path lined with flowers. Roses. Daisies. Daffodils. Lilies. Some she didn't recognize. Blooms in every color of the rainbow.

A white gazebo appeared in front of them. Flowers entwined around every pillar and covered the dome at the top. Ryder led her up two shallow steps to an altar within.

The cotton candy vendor stood behind the altar holding a Bible. Dressed in a long white robe, he looked like a minister now, but his face was unmistakable. Beautiful smile and shining crystal-blue eyes.

To the left stood the woman she'd seen on the boardwalk. To the right, another woman with long black hair. She'd never seen her before. Both women were also dressed in white and very beautiful. They turned and bade them in with a wave of their hands.

"You wish to marry?" the minister asked.

"We do," Ryder said.

"Then come forward."

Ryder faced her and stood motionless. "I love you. This is what I've always wanted. I knew from the second I saw you in the park."

"I love you, too. I want to be yours forever." Overwhelmed with happiness, her heart leapt.

The minister cleared his throat.

Ryder grinned and nodded his head toward the altar, then led her there.

"I've already heard your vows," the minister said. "You spoke them in your hearts long ago, and now you've said them again for the witnesses to hear. I therefore pronounce you husband and wife."

A candle on the altar lit by itself and flickered, but its light paled to the brilliance surrounding them. Light radiated from the minister himself.

"What about the ring?" Ryder asked him.

"Oh, yes. The ring." The man smiled and nodded to the black-haired woman.

She took Ryder's hand, then leaned in and whispered in his ear. Then she kissed him on the cheek.

Strangely, she looked a lot like him.

He turned to Amber. "I give you this ring as a token of my love and faithfulness."

He slipped it onto her finger. A solitary diamond sparkled in the sunlight. Amber's heart beat strong. *Stronger than ever.*

She gazed at the ring. "But I don't have one for you."

The woman beside her tapped her on the shoulder. "Yes you do, Ambie."

Amber gasped. Only one person had ever called her that. "Grandma?"

"Yes, my dear." She cupped her cheek with her hand. "Take this. Your grandpa wants you to have it." She pressed a silver band into Amber's palm.

Amber blinked away tears, then faced Ryder. "I give you this ring as a token of my love and faithfulness." She pushed it onto his finger.

"Very well, then," the minister said. "*Now* I pronounce you husband and wife." He chuckled. "Ryder, you may kiss your bride."

"Thank you."

He hesitated, looking at her with so much love it spilled from him. Then his lips touched hers. They moved so slow that the kiss seemed to last an eternity. She closed her eyes and savored it. Loved the *feel* of him. She became lost in it.

As her eyes opened, everything changed.

They stood in the center of a deep forest. Tall pine trees surrounded them. The scent made her smile.

It smells like Christmas.

She faced an enormous A-framed log house. "I've seen this before. I always wanted to see what it was like inside." She and her mom had passed it many times when they'd driven around the lake. She'd only been able to see the peak of it from the road, but then saw pictures of it when it was featured in a local magazine.

My dream home.

"Now's your chance." Ryder took her hand. They walked up a row of stone steps covered in red and pink rose petals.

Her heart thumped. "Are we really married?"

"Look at your hand."

Yes.

She lifted it into the sunlight, and the ring glistened. They'd finally be able to take their love to the next step. To experience what she'd only imagined. To lose herself in him.

He pushed the door open. They followed a path of rose petals that led them inside.

A white grand piano caught her eye. Memories of long ago when her mom used to play, rushed in. Their piano hadn't been anything like this one. Just an old second-hand upright she'd bought from a neighbor, then sold when Amber got sick.

She crossed to the instrument and ran her hand over the smooth lacquered finish. Then she glided her fingers along the keys. The sound brought back even more memories. Her mom used to dust the piano in the mornings. The tin-kling noise would wake her up.

"Do you play?" Ryder asked.

"Mom had started to teach me, but ... no."

He grinned and nodded to the bench. "Go on. Maybe you'll surprise yourself."

She looked down at her hands. Still as ever. She clenched her fists. Strong. Able.

After she tucked the long dress under her bottom, she moved onto the seat. She placed her hands on the keys and took a large breath.

Somehow, her fingers knew where to go. The melody filled the room. She glanced up at Ryder, while her hands kept moving.

He grinned. "Isn't that the theme from *The Young and the Restless*?"

She laughed. "Yep. My mom used to be a soap opera junkie."

"Mine, too." He leaned against the piano. "You play great."

"Not sure how. But I love it." Like second nature, her hands mastered the keys. She closed her eyes and let the music permeate her body. As the song came to an end, she quivered, knowing what would happen next.

Ryder took her hand and lifted her to her feet. "Abso-lutely beautiful."

She tilted her head toward the piano. "Yeah, it's a great song."

"That's not what I'm talking about. Though I liked *it*, too." He pulled her close and framed her face with his hands. "My wife. Beautiful inside and out." He kissed her slowly, then stood fully upright, breathing hard.

"I love you, Ryder," she rasped. "I'm ready."

They followed the trail of rose petals to an enormous bed.

Silently, they stared at each other.

"There's nothing to be afraid of," he whispered.

"I know. I'm *not* afraid."

He drew her close and caressed her back. His tiny kisses dotted her face. She shut her eyes tight and concentrated on the feel of his hands and the softness of his kisses.

When she opened them, she found herself alone at the foot of the bed.

Her breath caught. *What happened?*

Ryder cleared his throat, and she let out a soft laugh. Her wonderful new husband lay in the bed under the covers propped up on pillows.

"I'm waiting," he said. His voice sounded extra low.

And so sexy.

His better-than-fantastic arms were above the covers as well as most of his bare chest.

Her heart raced. "Close your eyes," she whispered. "And *don't* peek."

With a grin, he obeyed.

She quickly removed her clothes, then lifted the blankets and climbed in beside him. The soft bed embraced them.

Skin on skin, she nestled against him.

"It won't get dark here, will it?" she asked, looking around the room.

"Nope." He shook his head, eyes filled with love. "Never again."

"Maybe one day I won't be so nervous taking off my clothes in front of you."

"You have nothing to be worried about. You're amazing." He ran his hand along her side. It coasted along her curves. "I peeked."

"You!" She thumped him on the chest, then lay her head against it.

"Sorry. Couldn't help myself." He took large breaths that made his chest rise and fall beneath her.

She propped herself up to look at his face. *The most handsome man in the world.* But then his eyes shifted from hers and peered downward.

Her face heated.

I know what you're looking at.

"Don't blush, Amber. Your body's incredible. I like to look at it."

"You're pretty amazing yourself." She grinned. "My ape man." She rose up even higher to kiss him.

Their tongues danced together and sparked something more. He rolled her onto her back, and she gazed up at him, heart racing.

Go ahead.

He moved onto her and rested his legs between hers. She had no doubt he wanted her.

Yes.

With his muscular arms, he held himself up and hovered above her. "I never dreamed I'd be able to do this." He breathed so hard. As if he'd run a hundred miles. "I'm going to make love to you."

She licked her lips and nodded.

I want you to.

He kissed the tip of her nose. "I won't hurt you."

"I know." His firm body sent a rush of heat deep into her belly. "But that's just it." She raked her fingers through his hair. "You're only a dream. I know you can't hurt me physically. But I'm afraid I'll wake up, and you'll be gone again. My heart can't take it."

"Then don't sleep, Amber. Don't sleep ..." He buried his head against her, kissed her neck, then worked his way to her lips.

Their hands freely wandered. They caressed and explored each other. Amber discovered new sensations she'd never seen in movies. How could she? Seeing was one thing, but feeling was so much more.

And just as their mouths learned their own language of love, their bodies did the same. They joined together in passion and love. Not a bit of pain, only pleasure.

* * *

Fear gripped Amber so hard she didn't want to open her eyes. They'd made love for hours. Or maybe it had only been moments. Time seemed nonexistent.

She'd known last night her time was short, and death was close. She'd hardly been able to breathe or talk to her mom. But at least she'd been able to spend a final night with Ryder. To know what it felt like to love him. *Completely* love him. With her heart *and* her body.

He'd been gentle, but passionate, and she'd opened up to him and gave him all she could give.

But I want more. I want him forever.

"Did you sleep well?"

Her heart pattered faster.

She opened her eyes and flipped over in the bed.

"Good morning, my love."

Ryder kissed her. A soft, sweet kiss.

She grabbed onto him and kissed him harder, then threw herself on top of him and kissed him again.

He laughed. "I thought you had enough already."

"Never." She decided to prove it.

It grew into something greater than each time before. Waking up with him affirmed she could stay.

Fearless, she let herself go.

Ryder flopped back onto the sheets and let out an exhausted breath. "Wow! At least I know it's impossible to kill me." He grinned, then pushed a strand of hair from her face.

"What do you mean?"

"You still don't understand, do you?"

"Guess not."

Amber jerked, startled by an enormous white cat that jumped onto the bed. It padded its way up until it reached her face, then pawed at her nose.

She cocked her head, then sat up and pulled the blankets around her body. "Snowdrop?"

"*Snowdrop?*" Ryder chuckled. "Odd name. Why not Snow*flake?*"

Amber fingered the snowflake-shaped tag on the cat's pink collar. "I was six when I named her. I was confused. But the name stuck."

Ryder stroked the cat's long fur. "She's beautiful. The name suits her."

"But, she can't be real. She died when I was twelve. Right before I got sick."

She covered her mouth. She'd never told him she'd been sick. But somehow, it didn't seem to matter anymore.

He looked at her with his loving brown eyes, but didn't comment. Maybe he'd known all along.

"She's real, Amber," he said, then kissed her. "As real as you and me."

A heavy knock on the door startled her. Even more so than the cat.

"Someone's at the door?" She stared at Ryder. "Weird." Why would anyone be bothering them *now*?

"Come in," he called out, then readjusted her blanket to fully cover her.

The dark-haired woman peered inside. "It's time."

He nodded and she left.

"What does she mean?" Amber couldn't take much more.

"We have to go." He threw back the covers and stood. Draped in a long white robe, he extended his hand.

She rose from the bed and she, too, was dressed in white.

Hand-in-hand they walked bare-footed out the door.

The forest had vanished, replaced by indescribable brilliance. Radiant light in multiple colors shone from every surface. Shades of red, blue, green, yellow, and violet surrounded a golden tree. But the colors were so brilliant—so pure—they weren't like anything she'd seen before. Beyond the tree shone an even brighter light.

The minister stood beside the tree holding the reins of their horses. To each side of the horses were their witnesses.

"Nothing to fear ever again," Ryder said. He took her hand and kissed it.

Warmth flooded over her. It started at the top of her head and moved down her body all the way to her bare feet.

Red nail polish. Just like Grandma's.

Grandma. She'd revealed herself at their wedding, but Amber had still believed it to be a dream. Didn't believe it could actually be her. The truth suddenly became clear.

She looked Ryder in the eye. "I died, didn't I?"

"*We* died." He stroked her face. "We won't be apart again."

She'd never been afraid to die. Always knew something better waited for her. She only feared being without *him*.

No more fear.

She clutched his arm as they approached the horses.

Her grandma smiled. "My sweet Ambie."

Still dazed, she approached the woman timidly. "But ... the man in my dream called you Anna. Just like the little girl I saw in other dreams. Why?"

"It's my name."

"I thought it was Jo."

"People called me Jo as I aged. It was all you ever heard. But I was born, Joanna."

"So you were the little girl chasing the puppy?"

"Yes. I loved that dog. And he comes to me now, whenever I want to see him." She drew Amber into a warm embrace. "You've been given a precious gift, Ambie."

Amber nodded. "Real love."

"Yes. Here, it's everywhere. But Ryder was in your heart even before time began. You were always meant to be."

"Like you and Grandpa."

"Yes. He's waiting to see you on the other side. What you've seen here while dreaming is a dark shadow compared to what lies beyond."

"But it's beautiful here. *Perfect.*"

"Just you wait and see." Her grandma beamed, then gestured to the mare. "Get on up now."

Amber mounted, and her grandma placed Snowdrop in her arms.

Ryder had been speaking to the pretty dark-haired woman. She hugged him and gave him a kiss, then he mounted the black horse. "I'll see you again soon, Mom."

"My little cowboy." She blew him a kiss, then looked at Amber. "I always knew the two of you would find each other." A bright smile made her even more beautiful.

Of course. No wonder they resembled each other. Amber's heart danced with happiness for him. She returned his mother's smile, then kept her horse still, waiting until Ryder came up beside her.

"Ambie, my dear?" Her grandma laid a hand on her leg.

"Yes?"

"There's someone else waiting to see you." She pointed to where they'd be going.

Something tickled Amber's neck, and she grasped it. Her fingers entwined around the silver chain, and the heart-shaped locket sparkled in the never-ending light.

She gasped. "Dad?" Even if she hadn't seen a single photo of him, she'd have known him anywhere. He stood there in the distance waiting for her with open arms.

Ryder moved in close. "Let's meet him together."

"Together forever," she said, and they rode off into the light.

Epilogue

Carol Stewart could barely stand. Everything weighed her down. It was still too fresh—her emotions raw. Her eyes were so clouded it had been a miracle she'd made it to the grave.

A dusting of snow hid any sign it had been recently dug. Two days old.

She'd had the headstone placed months ago, but they'd not had time to add the date of death.

She clutched the heart-shaped locket at her neck. Its mate lay six feet under her, strung around the neck of her only child.

Her legs buckled, and she dropped to the ground. Tears bubbled up and spilled over. She couldn't stop them. She sobbed. Wailed. Yelled at God. Shook her fists at the world for taking her daughter.

"It's not fair!"

Amber had tried to get her ready for this.

How could I be prepared to lose my child?

Even when she'd died peacefully with an angelic smile on her face. She'd looked so beautiful. But then, she stopped breathing. Carol tried everything to rouse her. She'd shaken her. *Hard.* She'd wanted to bring her back from wherever she'd gone. And when Amber just laid there limply in her arms, no matter what she did, Carol went into a fit of rage. The hospice nurse had to call in a doctor to sedate her.

Don't be afraid. I know I'm going someplace better.

Amber's words should give her comfort, but they haunted her. Her precious girl had been so strong. Fearless. Dealt with pain head-on.

"I'm the weak one, Amber." She sniffled and dug into her pocket for a tissue, but couldn't find a single one. She'd been going through box after box. When would it end?

"Miss?"

She looked up and attempted to bring him into view. A man waving a tissue.

"Here," he said. "Take it."

Sniffling again, she took it from his hand, but then turned back to the grave and resumed crying. A single tissue couldn't stop the tears.

Instead of leaving, he knelt beside her. "I'm sorry for your loss."

She blinked hard to rid her eyes of the water obstructing her view. Tears trickled down her cheeks. "Thank you." She sucked in air and blinked again.

"Is there anything I can do for you? I mean ..." He shook his head and stood. "Sorry."

She studied him a little more closely. A tall man with broad shoulders and a kind face. His long wool coat had been buttoned high to his neck, and a red knit scarf encircled it. Once her vision became clear, she noticed he, too, had puffy eyes.

Unable to stand, she remained on the ground, even though the cold penetrated her skin. "Don't be sorry. You were being kind."

"I'm not good at this."

"Is anyone?"

He pulled a cloth handkerchief from his coat pocket and dabbed at his eyes. "I don't know why I thought I could help. I'm not much good for anything right now." He stared upward as if searching the sky for something he'd lost.

"Me neither." She brushed the newly-fallen snow from Amber's name.

"Amber?" The man's tenor voice spoke her name like a clap of thunder.

"Yes. My daughter. She ..." Could she say it? "She died last week. Buried her two days ago." Her chin quivered, and the tears rolled.

A deep sob leapt from the man's chest, startling her. She gazed up at him. His hands covered his face.

She managed to push herself up from the ground. "You lost someone, too. Didn't you?"

He nodded into his hands. "My son. Last week as well." He lowered his hands and looked at her. "I don't know what I'm doing. I have a daughter at home who needs me, but I'm ... I'm broken. I just don't ..."

"I'm so sorry." Her heart ached for this stranger, sharing a similar pain. At least he wasn't *completely* alone.

"Thank you." He pulled his shoulders back, then blew his nose. "I'm a mess. Men aren't supposed to cry."

"*Bullshit.*" The moment she said the word, she laughed. "Amber would've loved to hear me say that. I fussed at her all the time for swearing."

He blew out a long breath. "I got onto my son, too. About stupid little things. I almost hate myself for it now. But isn't that what parents are supposed to do?"

"Yeah." Regret had been wearing on her. Why hadn't she been more patient? More understanding? The loving mother Amber needed? "We do the best we can."

"It's odd—meeting you like this. The last few months of my son's life were incredibly hard. The only comfort he got was in his dreams. And please don't take this wrong, but ... he told me about a girl he'd dreamed. Her name was Amber."

"Why would I take it wrong? Maybe they knew each other from school. Though she hadn't gone to public school for years. All her friends abandoned her when she got sick. Except for one."

"No. He didn't go to public school at all. My wife homeschooled him."

"She must be devastated."

He closed his eyes. "She died six years ago."

"Oh, God. I'm sorry. So it's just you and your daughter now?"

He silently nodded. "Ryder had a terrible time coping with her death. You see, he was a paraplegic—"

"Did you say, *Ryder*?"

"Yes. I know it's unusual, but ..." He grabbed her arm. "You don't look well. You're horribly pale."

Luckily he had hold of her or she'd be on the ground. "Did your son have dark hair and brown eyes? About six feet tall. And ... a *tattoo* on his right arm?"

He cocked his head, and his brows drew in. "Y—es."

"Are you from Colorado?"

He warily nodded.

Carol covered her mouth. "I need to sit down."

With a tight grip on her elbow, he led her to a bench. "How'd you know all that?"

"From Amber. She claimed to have met him in her dreams. Said he seemed real." Her mind spun, recalling every detail. "The night before she died she told me she loved him. That she wanted to be with him. Even said he wanted to marry her. She'd been in horrible pain that final week." She twisted the tissue into knots. "Cancer's so damn cruel."

He stared at her, saying nothing. His eyes filled with tears until they spilled over and ran down his face. "Cancer? The girl he mentioned wasn't sick. But he told me he loved her. Said she was sassy and cute. Short with big feet and long brown hair." He wiped his eyes with his coat sleeve. "He said in his dreams he could walk. Run. Swim." His face contorted, revealing much deeper pain. "Even rode a horse. Did all the things he'd not been able to for years. And in every dream she was there, sharing it all with him."

Carol gaped at him. "I came into her room one day, and she had her covers off looking at her feet. She asked me if I thought they were big." She clutched her chest, unable to comprehend everything he'd said. *How?* "Do you think ... I mean. Could it be possible?"

"I don't know what to think." He looked around the cemetery, then took an enormous breath. "I'd like to know everything about her. Would you tell me?"

"Only if you tell me about your son."

"Of course. You like coffee?"

"I like hot chocolate better."

He stood and extended his hand. "Oh. Wait." He pulled it to himself.

"What's wrong?"

"I didn't ask if you're married. It wouldn't be appropriate if—"

"I'm ..." She swallowed the lump in her throat. "I'm a widow." She held up her hand ...

He took it.

ACKNOWLEDGMENTS

When my son was in grade school, there was a girl several years older than him who had terminal cancer. As a young mom, I couldn't comprehend what her parents were feeling, or how they managed to face each day. The girl continued on in school until she became too sick, then they took her home and cared for her until she died.

So young to die and not be able to experience all that life has to offer. That's what inspired *He's in My Dreams*. I wanted to give Amber her dearest wish.

In my heart, I have no doubt that there's more for us than life here on Earth. I believe something beautiful and wonderful is waiting. Something we can't fully grasp until we pass from here. I pray this book will bring hope to others, and spark conversation between parents and children. Or maybe between best friends, like Amber and Stephanie, who helped each other cope.

My first thank you goes out to Melissa Chambers and Joy Dent. Fellow authors who gave it a test read. They encouraged me to move forward with it. Because I normally write historical women's fiction, I hadn't been up on what was trending in *young adult* fiction, so until Melissa told me, I didn't have a clue there was another book about a girl with cancer currently on the market. It had everyone talking. But she assured me my story wasn't anything like it, so I kept on. I'm glad I did. I feel Amber's story needed to be told.

Before finalizing the manuscript, I wanted to be certain my research was accurate. I spoke to a friend who works in the medical field and asked her if she knew of an oncologist who'd be willing to answer some questions for me. Thank you, Joann Caughron, for leading me to Dr. Patrick Williams. And thank you, Dr. Williams, for taking the time to meet with me and answer my list of questions. Your insight helped me understand the difficulties Amber faced. And even from our brief meeting, I could tell you have a gentle spirit. You're the kind of doctor any person facing something so horrible would be comforted to have by their side. A true blessing.

Sadly, I had my own experience with a patient in hospice care. I tended my mother-in-law before she passed from Alzheimer's disease. Some incredible things happened during those five months with her. Some of which I'll be writing about in another book. I often got the feeling she had one foot at home, and the other in Heaven. Something else that inspired Amber's story.

Once I completed this book, I had a number of other Beta readers who helped me. Thank you Birgit Barnes, Bobbie Bauer, Mary Ann Brooks, Lisa Eaton, Diane Gardner, Jennifer Gatlin, Kim Gray, Stacy O'Brien, and Sarah Smith-Vanek.

A special thanks to Kim's daughter, Mikenzie Gray, who helped with some of my wording. Having a teen's insight when writing about teens is invaluable.

I spent many wonderful years in Coeur d'Alene, Idaho, so it was fun writing about a place I knew well. The experience Amber and Ryder had riding up Sherman Avenue to Playland Pier came from my memory. I'll never forget the excitement of seeing the Ferris wheel rising above the sparkling water. And, I have fresher memories of singing on the floating stage at the Coeur d'Alene Resort.

For my Coeur d'Alene readers, I hope I did your beautiful city justice. And for you *older* Cd'A readers, I hope you enjoyed stepping back in time.

Thank you to my mom, Janet Launhardt, and my aunt, Judy Reynolds, for reading this before publication and giving me feedback. Your familiarity to the locations and settings in this story helped me make it real.

I'm thrilled to have been led to Alicia Dean, who edited this book and gave me a good grasp on enhancing the relationship between Amber and her mother. Thank you also to Rae Monet who found my perfect Ryder and created a beautiful cover. Thank you to Jesse Gordon for formatting, and keeping my words on the page.

Finally, thank you readers! I'd love to hear from you. You'll find links to my website and Facebook page at the end of this book.

Other Books by Jeanne Hardt

The River Romance Series:

Marked

Tainted

Forgotten

From the Ashes of Atlanta

A Golden Life

The Southern Secrets Saga:

Deceptions

Consequences

Desires

Incivilities

For more information about Jeanne's books,
check out the links below:

www.facebook.com/JEANNEHARDTAUTHOR
www.jeannehardt.com
www.amazon.com/author/jeannehardt
www.goodreads.com/jeannehardt

Made in the USA
Columbia, SC
08 September 2021

45121408R00174